"Thank you," she said as she walked over to the chair and sat down, adjusting the robe's belt around her waist. She felt self-conscious at being so undressed in front of him, but she was glad she wasn't alone in the room. Her mind was racing, trying to think of something to say to him to keep him in the room with her. But the only thing she could think about was the way his muscular arms looked in his shirt and how a trickle of perspiration was making its way down his brow toward his finely shaped nose. She wanted to wipe it away, but shook her head instead, chiding herself for having thoughts about him at such a time.

"Anything else you need, Mrs. Watkins?"

"It's Ms. Watkins. Please, call me Marcia."

"All right, anything else you need, ma'am?"

"Uh—no."

Walter nodded and started to walk to the door. Marcia stood quickly.

"Wait!"

Walter turned to look at her. "Yes…?"

A LOVER'S LEGACY

VERONICA PARKER

Genesis Press, Inc.

Indigo Love Stories

An imprint of Genesis Press, Inc.
Publishing Company

Genesis Press, Inc.
P.O. Box 101
Columbus, MS 39703

ISBN: 1-58571-167-5
Manufactured in the United States of America

First Edition

Visit us at www.genesis-press.com
or call at 1-888-Indigo-1

DEDICATION

To Christian, my love.

ACKNOWLEDGMENTS

I'd like to thank the staff at Genesis Press, especially Angelique Justin and Sidney Rickman, and to all my fans, thank you.

CHAPTER ONE

Marcia was exhausted. As she drove her late model Chrysler into the driveway of the two-story townhouse, she struggled to stifle a yawn. She had spent the past three months working around the clock trying to finish the new home for Dr. and Mrs. Trai Baker. *That Baker woman…she's enough to drive anyone crazy with her fussiness.* Everything had to be perfect. *Dr. Baker's a saint for having to deal with that woman on a daily basis.*

However, she had managed to please Mrs. Baker and after her months of hard work, Gloria Baker had paid Marcia's hefty fee. Marcia was now looking forward to going home and spending a few days relaxing before beginning her next project.

She parked her car and yawned. The thought of having a nice hot bath was the first thing that popped into her mind as she made her way to the front door.

As soon as she put the key into her door lock, she heard the sound of a ringing telephone. *Damn…not going to make it.* She hurried to unlock the door and then calmed herself. She was always hurrying around, tense, afraid she would miss a client's call. Today she was just too tired to hurry. Besides, given the success of her work at the exclusive Baker home, her phone would likely be ringing off the hook. The residents of Manchester, Vermont, always hired designers by word of mouth and she was quite sure that Gloria Baker would give her a good recommendation.

She smiled to herself as she opened the door and calmly entered the hallway. The phone had stopped ringing. Marcia placed her keys on the hallway table and was about to take off her coat when it started ringing again.

Must be important if they're calling again. She walked over and picked up the phone in the living room.

"Hello?"

"Hey there, sister."

Marcia sighed, exasperated. Her twenty-five-year-old sister, Anna, had moved down to New Orleans two years previously to get a degree in music appreciation, but had dropped out soon after and had found work as a cocktail waitress in one of the jazz lounges in the French Quarter. She had a beautiful voice and hoped to get a chance to sing in a nightclub, but the opportunity had yet to present itself. She'd called a few months before to ask for money because she couldn't make her rent. It was expensive to live in the Quarter, but Anna had decided to rent a room there so she could be around "influential people."

"How's it going?"

"Fine. Why haven't you called?"

"The phone works both ways, you know," Anna said.

"I know," Marcia said, sitting down on her sofa. "I'd use it, too, if I knew where you were staying week to week. Which I don't, by the way."

"You know it's hard to find a roommate in this city. Besides, I've *only* moved four times in the past year."

"Try seven."

"Okay, seven."

"What's up? Something must have happened if you're calling me."

"It has."

"Oh no. You didn't get fired, did you?"

"No."

"Do you need money? I can send—"

"Marcia. Stop, please, and listen to me."

"Okay."

"I didn't get fired. I'm not in trouble. It's good news actually."

"Oh my God! You've landed a singing gig finally. Oh Anna…"

"No," Anna sighed. "It doesn't have to do with singing. I'm not thinking about that anymore, actually."

"You're not thinking about singing anymore?"

"No, I've got other interests."

"Since when? You've wanted to be a singer since…"

Anna sighed again. "Do you want to hear my news or not?"

"All right. What is it?"

"It's just you don't have to worry about me anymore."

"Oh no?" Marcia asked sarcastically.

"Yup. I've found a permanent residence."

Marcia sat up. "Permanent? Where? And with whom?"

"Well," Marcia could hear excitement in Anna's voice, "with my soon-to-be *husband!*"

"What?" Marcia screamed into the phone.

"I'm engaged!"

Marcia stood up, upsetting the phone cradle. "You're what?"

"Yes," Anna said, her excitement coming through the phone. "The wedding is next week. I am going to be Mrs. Justin St. Jean."

"Oh my God!"

"And I want you to be my maid of honor. Will you, Marcia? You're the best friend I have in the whole world."

"Of course I will. I'd be honored, but who is he? And what's all the rush to get married?" Marcia asked suspiciously as she picked up the phone cradle and set it back onto the coffee table. "Oh, God, you're not pregnant, are you?"

"No…" Her sister's voice was irritated. "Justin asked me last night. He says he doesn't want a long engagement."

"Why not?"

"He doesn't want to wait for me to be his wife."

"How long have you been dating him?"

"Two months…"

"Two months!"

"Oh, God, Marcia…please be happy for me. I love him so much."

"I am happy, Anna. It's just that I don't want you to rush into anything. You know Mom and Dad wouldn't want you to rush into anything." Marcia glanced at the photo of her parents sitting beside the phone. Tom and Carol Watkins had been killed in a car accident ten years earlier. In their will, they had made her Anna's guardian and she had gone to extreme lengths to make sure that Anna had grown up happy and safe. She had protested greatly when Anna had decided to move down to New Orleans to attend college and disapproved when Anna dropped out to pursue singing, waiting tables part-time.

But it had always been Anna's dream to be a singer and in the past two years, Anna had sounded happy and said she really felt that she belonged in a city like New Orleans. She loved jazz music and the nightlife and her job at a local spot called the Louis Armstrong. But Marcia could not help worrying about her much younger, and in her mind, impressionable sister.

"I know what you're thinking. Stop worrying so much. I'm not a little kid anymore. I'm a woman, and in about a week, I'll be a married woman."

Marcia took off her heels and flung them onto the carpet. "But I don't know anything about him. Who is this Justin St. Jean? You've never even mentioned him before now."

"Oh, Marcia," Anna gushed, and it was all Marcia could do to not be overcome by the sickening sweetness, "we met at a piano bar exactly two months to the day he asked me to be his wife."

"How romantic."

"Isn't it? It was love at first sight. He's so gorgeous and he treats me like a queen. You're going to love him."

"I'm sure I will," Marcia said, sitting back down. "That is, when I meet him."

"You're going to meet him tomorrow."

"Tomorrow?"

"I'm getting married *next week* or didn't you hear me?"

"Next week? I didn't hear that part. Lord Anna, you just got engaged. You haven't even had an engagement party and here you are talking about walking down the aisle."

"We want to be married as soon as possible and I need you down here to help me with planning the wedding. Plus, I want you to meet his family. They really like me and they're going to like you, too."

"Tomorrow? I can't leave tomorrow. I have a business or did you forget?"

"Please, Marcia. I need you."

"If I had time to get someone to cover for me maybe, but—"

"You're the boss. You can take time off."

Marcia sighed. She hated arguing with Anna. "All right, I guess I can."

"Great. I've already booked a ticket for you. You leave out of Burlington tomorrow afternoon and arrive into Louis Armstrong International Airport at three-thirty P.M. Justin is sending a car for you."

"My God. You've already arranged everything, I see. Whatever happened to my disorganized little sister?"

"She's all grown up."

"I see that," Marcia said, her head spinning. "You don't have to convince me. I'll be there. But next time you decide to get married, please give me some advance warning. Perhaps more than a day to get my business covered and pack."

Anna laughed. "I don't plan on getting married again. He's the one."

"I hope so," Marcia said softly to herself.

"Don't worry about getting a dress for the wedding or anything. We'll go shopping for dresses when you get here. Just throw some things into a bag and I'll see you tomorrow afternoon. You're just going to love New Orleans."

"I'm sure I will," Marcia replied, unconvinced.

"See you tomorrow. I love you."

"I love you, too, Anna. I'm very happy for you."

"Thanks. Bye!"

Anna hung up. Marcia slowly replaced the phone and leaned back against the sofa. Her little sister was getting married. She shook her head in disbelief. It was all so sudden, but Anna seemed so happy that she couldn't help feeling happy for her.

But as she thought about packing and getting her business phone covered for the next week or so, she felt her heart sink. Here she was, a thirty-seven-year-old woman with a successful business; yet, she was all alone. No husband or boyfriend, or even a lover she could hand things over to. Certainly no man to accompany her to her own sister's wedding. She couldn't count all the events she'd gone to alone in the past ten years. It was getting to be more than even she could bear sometimes. Her happy "I'm an independent woman and loving it" smile didn't last long in rooms filled with happily married women. The truth of the matter was that she was lonely, real lonely.

She sighed and fiddled with the bun at the back of her head. There was no one to blame for her isolation but herself. She had always put work as a priority before friends and especially before love. The truth was that she was a confident and self-assured woman, except when it came to men. Around attractive men, she found herself struggling for words and often felt like a twelve-year-old schoolgirl, unsure and shy. So she would try to compensate for her shyness by talking non-stop, often about silly subjects like the weather or the cost of gas. Most men were put off by her businesslike attitude and found her intimidating or, she hated to admit, boring. She knew that, to the contrary, she was interesting, but she could never bring out that side of her personality during a date, no matter how hard she tried.

She untied her hair and let the curly black tresses fall around her face. As she ran her hand at the back of the bun, she could feel the dry strands underneath her fingertips. *I'll have to wash and set it tonight. There won't be time tomorrow.* Again she yawned and tried to think about how happy Anna had sounded on the phone, but it was difficult. That familiar sadness that she lived with began to fill her heart and her mind. It was easier to tell herself that she had never found "Mr. Right" than to admit that she was alone because she had let herself be alone. She had never been in love and sadly, no one had ever been in love with her. As she stood and walked to the hall mirror, her reflection glared back at her.

At five feet, ten inches tall, she was a big girl, but well proportioned. She had dark eyes, the color of deep chocolate, which complemented her chocolate-colored skin. She had always been attractive enough, but her sister had inherited their mother's silky skin and long, raven hair, hazel eyes, and voluptuous figure.

As Marcia turned to inspect her own figure in the mirror, she saw that her body was still firm. She had a full bust and thick hips, though, and no amount of exercise could help that little extra bit on her rear end, but she thought she was what was called "attractive." *So why doesn't anyone want me?*

As turning forty loomed just around the corner, Marcia was beginning to worry that she would never find someone and she desperately wanted to become a wife and mother. She sighed as she picked up the phone and searched for her personal phone book in her purse. Her work gave her joy and fulfilled her…almost. *Almost.* As she dialed her office, she again sighed.

It seemed as if she was destined to always be alone.

CHAPTER TWO

The next morning, Marcia found herself in a first class seat on her way to New Orleans. When the check-in girl had told her she would be sitting in first class, Marcia had disagreed vehemently. Then the girl showed her the reservation and she saw that a first class ticket had indeed been purchased for her. Shock didn't begin to describe her reaction. *Where did Anna get that kind of money?* She was immediately suspicious, and sitting in that luxurious seat did not ease her fears that Anna had fallen into something illegal. After all, what were they paying cocktail waitresses these days?

When a flight attendant tapped her on the shoulder, Marcia practically jumped out of her seat. "Yes!"

"Sorry to disturb you, ma'am, but would you like a drink before take off?"

"Uh, no." And then reconsidering, Marcia smiled and nodded. "Actually, yes. May I have a scotch and soda, please?"

"Certainly, ma'am."

As Marcia watched the flight attendant prepare her drink, she leaned back in the leather seat and began to relax. She shook her head and laughed. She was always jumping to conclusions. Anna's fiancé had probably chipped in to pay for the ticket. Who knew? This time, though, Marcia was determined to keep her usually suspicious temperament in check. *She's my only sister and it's her special time.*

The flight attendant handed her the drink and a pack of peanuts. "Here you are, ma'am. Enjoy your drink. After takeoff, we will be serving a complimentary lunch. Would you like steak or chicken?"

Marcia smiled and sipped her drink. "Chicken, please."

As the flight attendant walked away, Marcia opened the peanuts and took a sip of her drink even as she thought she needed to lose some weight before the wedding. *I don't want to have to squeeze into some tiny maid of honor dress.*

She smiled as she recalled her parents' eating habits. They had not exactly been the poster family for good health. Her parents had been meat and potatoes people. Every night for dinner when Marcia was growing up there had been the usual three staple items: meat dish, potato dish, and maybe a tiny vegetable dish, perhaps green beans with butter. They'd had fish on Fridays and Sundays. Family dinners had always been filled with warmth and laughter.

Mom and Dad... She felt tears fill her eyes and she shut them as the captain announced that they were set for takeoff. Silently, Marcia prayed that her sister would be as happily married as their parents had been.

At exactly three-thirty local time, Marcia disembarked at Louis Armstrong International Airport. She suddenly saw a limousine driver holding a sign that read MARCIA WATKINS. She hurried over to the man and stuck out her hand.

"Hello, I'm Marcia Watkins."

The driver shook her hand politely, introduced himself as Marcus, and taking her suitcase, led her down the stairs to the curb outside. "This way please, ma'am."

Marcia followed the driver and was surprised to see a stretch limousine. "That's for me?"

"Yes, ma'am," Marcus said, holding the door open for her.

After Marcia hesitantly got in, he shut the door and walked to the trunk to place her suitcase inside. He then got into the driver's seat.

"You all right there, ma'am?"

"Yes, thank you." In fact, Marcia was more than comfortable. The roomy car had a bar, a television, and a CD player. The soft sounds of jazz music played in the background.

"I slipped in a Miles Davis CD. I hope you don't mind."

"No," Marcia said, "I love jazz."

"Good," he said, pulling out of the lane and onto the freeway, "then you're really gonna like this town."

Marcia smiled and sitting back, looked out the window. The airport was twenty minutes from downtown New Orleans and as Marcia watched first green fields and then office buildings and industrial warehouses pass by, she felt a fluttering in her stomach, a fluttering of excitement. She hadn't seen her sister in more than six months and she'd missed her. Even though Anna was getting married, she made a promise to herself to make an effort to see her more often.

When the limousine entered the French Quarter, Marcia was amazed at the diversity of the city. There were high rises and Starbucks coffee houses and then just as suddenly, quaint French style cafés, bars and two story buildings with balconies. Looking forward to spending a week here, she smiled to herself. She had already planned to take a riverboat cruise and try the pralines and po'boy sandwiches.

As they drove down Royal Street, Marcia admired the pretty streets with their wrought iron balconies. When Marcus stopped the limousine outside 1140 Royal Street, Marcia glanced up at a large, but rather plain gray mansion set amongst so many other quaint homes.

"Here we are, ma'am," Marcus said, opening the door for her.

"Is this Mr. St. Jean's home?" Marcia asked as she let Marcus help her out of the car.

"No, ma'am. He's got a home outside the city. He has an apartment in this building."

"Does he own the building?"

"No, ma'am," he answered as he walked toward the back of the car and popped the trunk. "Just an apartment in there. Nice place, I hear. Landlord's name is Mr. Dufrane."

Marcia was impressed by the driver's knowledge of the home. "You don't say."

He nodded as he carried Marcia's suitcase to the front door and rang the bell for apartment five. "I've been working for Mr. St. Jean for ten years now. You learn a few things here and there."

As Marcia stared up at the tall walls of the mansion, a slight chill spread across her back and her arms, even though it was more than 80 degrees outside. *Is this where I'll be staying?*

As if in answer to her question, the front door was suddenly opened and there stood Anna Watkins, her face aglow with excitement. Behind her stood an older man, who appeared to be in his forties, with dark eyes and graying hair. He watched Marcia carefully from behind large black spectacles.

"Marcia!" Anna screamed, throwing herself into Marcia's arms. "I've missed you so much!"

Marcia was practically suffocating from the intensity of the hug, but she held on. She'd missed Anna and could feel tears welling up in her eyes. Anna pulled away and looked at her. "You're not crying, are you? Stop it or else I'll start crying."

Marcia laughed, wiping at her eyes. "Let me take a look at you," she said, spinning Anna around. She took in Anna's elegant dress, her updo, her high-heeled Gucci shoes and matching handbag and was astonished. Her little sister had grown into a sophisticated woman. *Soon-to-be-married sophisticated woman.* Marcia turned to look at the man standing behind Anna.

His face was a bit strained and he held his arms tightly behind his back. He turned to the driver. "Marcus, thank you. We won't need your services until later this afternoon."

Marcus nodded politely, and getting inside the limousine, started the engine and drove away. When Marcia turned back to meet her sister's fiancé, his face had gone from strained to angry. She was startled for a moment, but as quickly as the anger had appeared, it disappeared and was replaced by a warm smile and handshake.

"It's a pleasure to finally meet you, Ms. Watkins. Anna has told me so much about you. She hardly slept a wink last night she was so excited about your arrival." He turned and placed an arm around Anna's waist.

Marcia smiled and returned the warm greeting. "It's nice to meet you, too, Mr. St. Jean. Anna has told me so much about you." She winked at Anna, who blushed.

"Please. Call me Justin. We're going to be family, aren't we?"

Marcia smiled and looked from Justin to Anna. Anna was positively glowing, but though he smiled, Marcia felt a sense of distance. *He's probably just nervous.* She looked at Justin carefully. He was a handsome man, a Creole with dark brown eyes, light skin and dark hair. But it was the age difference that had Marcia stumped. *He has to be at least twenty years older...*

But seeing the way Anna clung to him, Marcia could not doubt that her sister was in love. She had never seen Anna act like that with anyone.

"Shall we go inside, Ms. Watkins?" Justin said, pointing the way into the mansion.

"Please. Call me Marcia," Marcia said as Anna took her hand and the two women followed him inside. Justin turned in the elegant foyer and smiled at her. "All right, then, Marcia."

Marcia was overcome when she saw the interior of the home. The outside of the mansion was plain, given the affluent standards of the neighborhood, but the interior was exquisite. Chandeliers hung from the ceilings, Oriental carpets decorated the foyer and as Marcia peered into the lounge at the right, she saw a grand piano, leather couches and a fireplace that practically took up the whole room.

"This place is really beautiful," Marcia exclaimed, wandering into the lounge and admiring the paintings hanging on the wall.

"Thank you. Most visitors to LaLaurie Mansion are quite taken by its magnificence."

"And you own an apartment here?"

"Yes. There are eight private apartments in this mansion and an advisory board. The historical society next door helps to maintain the home and Mr. Dufrane, the landlord, is quite generous with both his time and expertise. He's lived here for more than fifteen years."

Anna beamed as she again hugged Marcia. "I'm so happy you're here, Marcia. This is going to be so much fun! This afternoon, we'll have a late lunch at Galatoire's and then maybe go shopping for a while and then tonight…"

"Darling…" Justin said, taking Anna's hand, "perhaps your sister would like to rest before you begin dragging her around the city."

Anna looked from Justin to Marcia. "Oh, I'm sorry, honey, I didn't mean to."

Marcia was surprised by her sister's quick acquiescence. Anna was not a person to be told what to do. *At least, she didn't used to be.* But Marcia smiled. Her sister was in love and was getting married, and Justin seemed nice enough.

"There's no need to fuss over me. I just need to freshen up. Is there somewhere I can wash my hands?" Marcia began.

"No, no, no! You're going to be staying in the apartment upstairs. Take some time to rest. You've had a long flight. Let me show you up." Justin picked up Marcia's suitcase, and walked toward the winding staircase that led into a grand hallway. Marcia looked up at a massive chandelier and then at the wall paintings. The manner of dress of the various subjects suggested that the paintings were from a different time. Marcia stopped in front of one of them, a portrait of a woman with pale skin and long dark hair neatly tied at the nape of her neck. She was dressed in a beautiful gown with white collar and wore jewels about her neck. However, there was something unsettling about her eyes.

"Who is that woman in the painting?" She pointed to the portrait.

Justin stopped and frowned. "Odd. Never seen that hanging there before."

"Do you know who she is?"

"Yes." Justin turned and smiled. "That's Madame Delphine LaLaurie. She was the mistress of this mansion back in the 1830s. She fell out with society, some sort of disgraceful business, and disappeared from New Orleans. Some say she went to France."

Marcia stared into the eyes of Madame LaLaurie, mesmerized. "There's just something about her eyes…"

Justin tilted his head and looked at the portrait. "I suppose. I wasn't aware you were interested in art. If you like, I can arrange a trip to the museum."

Marcia smiled and continued up the stairs. "That's kind of you. Maybe if we have time."

"Yes. If time permits."

They entered an elegant, long hallway. Marcia could see another set of stairs at the end of the hallway, but there was a door with a padlock and a sign: NO ADMITTANCE.

"Where does that staircase go?"

Justin glanced over at the door. "That leads to the third floor. The owner has a private study up there and I believe there is a storage room as well. I've never been up there. He and the landlord are the only ones with the key to the door."

"I see," Marcia replied. But there was something about that doorway that held her attention for a moment.

"Ah, here we are," Justin said as he set the suitcase down and unlocked the door to the apartment at the end of the hallway. Marcia followed Anna and Justin inside and was overcome by the opulence of the apartment. There was a tastefully designed living room and fireplace, a top of the line kitchen, a bathroom with marble bath, and two large bedrooms.

"This place is marvelous," Marcia said in shock, taking it all in. "Am I really going to be staying here?"

"Anna and I must return to my family's estate in Vacherie. It's our family home. But we thought you'd enjoy staying in the city, as this is your first visit. I hope you will be comfortable," Justin began.

"I'm sure I will, but this apartment is big enough for all of us, don't you think?" Marcia replied. She wandered into a bedroom and was overcome by the lavish furnishings and canopied bed.

Justin continued as if she hadn't spoken. "I assured Anna that you would be more comfortable staying here, in the heart of the French Quarter, or Vieux Carre as we call it here. Anna and I will be back and forth."

"Oh but—" Marcia began.

"Of course, if you're not happy with the arrangements, we could book a hotel." Justin replied. Marcia could see that he was just trying to be polite and didn't want to be a bother. "Oh, no, this place is terrific," Marcia said, hugging Anna to her. "It's just perfect. I'll feel like a queen."

"And we won't be too far away—" Anna began hesitantly.

"Your sister has already politely accepted the invitation to stay here, Anna. Nothing else needs to be said."

Marcia glanced over at Justin in surprise and then over at Anna. Anna looked nervous and apologetic. There was no need to admonish Anna, Marcia thought. She was about to say something to Justin when he suddenly nodded and taking Anna's arm, smiled at Marcia. "Then it's all arranged. Mr. Dufrane is across the hall if something isn't working properly. He's always here, but I should warn you, he is a bit of a recluse."

"Recluse?"

"He tends to keep to himself. Hardly see the man when I'm here. However, if something is wrong with the apartment, he will help, so don't worry." He handed Marcia a business card. "We're going to stop by my office on Bienville Street, just down the block. I've some work to do before we take our dinner. If you should need anything, feel free to call."

"Thank you, Justin. I'm sure I'll be fine."

"Then perhaps we should let your sister have a rest and come for her later," he said to Anna.

Anna turned to Marcia and they embraced. "I'm so happy you're here. Take a nap and we'll come by in a couple of hours and take you to dinner. We've got something special planned." Anna winked.

Marcia felt her anxiety over Justin's harshness to her sister melt away when she saw the joy on Anna's face. She was thrilled to see her sister so happy. They had had much sadness in their lives, and it was good to finally see Anna settling down and finding a home with someone she loved. After Marcia bid them good-bye and shut the door, she leaned against it, a mixture of excitement and sadness in her heart. If only she could find someone, if only she weren't so alone.

~

Later, after a soak in the marble bathtub and short nap, Marcia felt like a whole new woman. As she dressed, she was looking forward to a nice New Orleans'-style dinner and exploring the city. The window of her bedroom overlooked Royal Street and the bright lights and buzz of the French Quarter carried up to her room. There were French doors that led out to the balcony. *My own private balcony. I'll have to thank my sister for making the suggestion that I stay here.* She opened the French doors a bit and let in some fresh air. The weather was warm, breezy and inviting. Jazz music drifted in from nearby Bourbon Street and as she pulled on her black pants and matching blouse, she smiled to herself. She liked New Orleans already.

She then walked into the bathroom to fix her hair and makeup. The humidity was causing her curly hair to frizz and she applied both gel and hairspray to control the locks. She sighed, wishing she'd had the good fortune of being born with Anna's hair.

It was when she was slathering on her face cream that she first felt a hand on her shoulder. At first she thought she had imagined it, but then it happened again. Marcia spun around, thinking that perhaps someone had come into the room, but there was no one behind her. She was all alone. Turning back around, she shook her head. *I've just had a long day.* But then there it was again…a hand softly caressing her back. She shivered, but the feeling went away as quickly as it had come. Looking anxiously around the bathroom, she cautiously made her way through the apartment. "Hello, anyone here?"

Silence greeted her. *I really do need a vacation if I'm this high strung.* She laughed out loud and continued getting ready.

CHAPTER THREE

Justin and Anna picked Marcia up in a horse and carriage complete with driver.

Marcia laughed as she stepped out of the mansion. "What is all this?"

"It was Justin's idea. He thought that you'd like a carriage ride through the French Quarter before we go to dinner."

"That was very thoughtful. Thank you, Justin."

"My pleasure. Anything to see to your comfort and enjoyment while in our city." Justin, dressed in a dark blue Zegna suit, stepped out and helped Marcia into the carriage. He spread a blanket across her lap and then settling back against the seat, nodded to the driver. Marcia smiled at him, charmed by his gracious manners. He certainly is a Southern gentleman, she thought.

"How are you feeling, Marcia? Not too tired for some fine creole cooking after a turn around the Quarter?" Justin asked, taking Anna's hand and holding it. For the first time, Marcia noticed the size of her sister's engagement ring. *How come I didn't notice* that *before?* It was a two-carat diamond, set amongst a crest of gold and sapphires. It was magnificent and shown as bright as Anna's eyes.

"No, not tired at all, thank you. I had a nap. By the way Anna, you look great."

"Thanks. So do you."

Anna wore a soft velvet black gown and matching sandals. Marcia glanced down at her outfit. She was presentable, but her black pants and blouse simply did not stand up to what Justin and Anna were wearing. No matter, she thought. Anna had promised that they would go shopping for her maid of honor gown and she would pick up something formal in town.

"Let me see your ring," Marcia said. Anna thrust her hand forward willingly. Marcia took Anna's hand and inspected the ring. "It's beautiful."

"Isn't it?" Anna said, beaming at Justin. He sat back, a pleased look on his face. "Only the best for my darling," he said.

"Isn't Justin the most wonderful man in the world," Anna gushed.

Marcia nodded. "It certainly seems that way. Congratulations to you both."

"I couldn't have the future wife of a St. Jean wearing anything but the best." Justin turned to her. "Anna tells me you're not married."

Marcia was a bit taken aback by the statement. "No, I'm not."

There was an uncomfortable silence as Anna and Justin stared at her, expecting her to say something more. "I guess you can say I'm married to my career," Marcia said, trying to make a joke of it, although she felt a bit nonplussed. She didn't like advertising that she was alone.

"Anna tells me that you're an interior decorator."

"Yes, I have my own company," Marcia responded, thankful for the change of subject.

"Really?" Justin asked. "Do you enjoy your work?"

"Yes," Marcia began, "I started the company seven years ago, when I got tired of working for other people. I like working for myself, not having to answer to anyone, but there's the added pressure of being responsible for the company. It's a trade off, but one I like."

"I understand. I also own my own company," Justin said.

Marcia was pleased that they had something in common. "And what, if I may ask, do you do for a living?"

Justin smiled politely. "Let's just say I'm in real estate. Actually, my family owns several rental houses and apartment buildings throughout the city. I manage them and do quite well for myself." He patted Anna's knee. "You needn't worry, Marcia, your sister will be well provided for."

"I'm happy to hear that," Marcia replied. But she felt a strange feeling come over her as she watched Justin stroke Anna's knee.

"How did you meet Anna?" She turned to her sister. "Was she renting a place from you?"

"No. As a matter of fact, I do not make it a habit to date tenants."

"Oh?"

"I told you we met in a lounge, remember?" Anna asked.

Justin turned and smiled at Anna. "I saw this lovely young woman sitting alone at the bar. Getting up my nerve, I asked if I could join her…"

Anna beamed as she interrupted. "And I look up and see this gorgeous man. I almost fainted!"

"Darling, do let me finish," Justin admonished, and then gave Anna a conciliatory kiss on the cheek before continuing. "As soon as we began talking, I knew I was in love. You see, I lost my wife Tiffany five years ago to cancer and was ready to meet someone to share my life with. But none of the women I knew in New Orleans interested me. They were after my money, my name, or both. I wanted a woman who would love me, not my money, an honest woman. Fortune smiled upon me and led me to your sister."

"It all seems so sudden…," Marcia began before she could stop herself.

Anna gave her a hard look, but Justin patted her hand and smiled. "It has been a rather short courtship, two months really, but I've always believed that when you find the one you want to be with, you shouldn't waste time. I was never an advocate of a long engagement."

Marcia nodded politely, but was concerned her sister had not clearly thought out her decision to marry Justin. Certainly he was handsome, charming and well-to-do, but how much did her sister really know about him? Still, looking at the way Anna was looking at Justin, Marcia could see that her sister was very much in love. *I need to stop worrying…she'll be fine.*

Dusk was just settling in as the carriage turned onto Toulouse Street. The driver, Ernest, was an informative guide.

"This is the French Quarter, or the Vieux Carre. It dates from around the early 1700s when it was formed as a shipping town by the Spanish. The French gained control of the city after the Spanish and claimed the city for Louis XVI. The Great Fire of 1788 destroyed most of the buildings in the French Quarter and the entire Quarter had to be rebuilt, this time by the Spanish who were back in control. But you can see the Parisian influence in the wrought iron balconies and red French facades…"

As Ernest turned onto Bourbon Street, Marcia saw several drunken patrons streaming out onto the street, plastic to go cups in their hands.

"Isn't that illegal?" Marcia asked Justin, indicating the plastic cups filled with a pinkish alcoholic concoction.

"No, I'm afraid not. New Orleans is a twenty-four hour city. You can drink on the streets and some of the bars never close," Justin said.

Marcia was surprised. "Never?"

"That's right."

Marcia sat back and pulled the blanket in around her legs. There was a night chill in the air. As she watched the oil street lamps turn on as if by magic, she was amazed at the beauty and magic of the Vieux Carre. It was a perfect blend of the historical and the modern.

"If you don't mind my asking, Justin, you don't sound like you're from the South."

Both Justin and the driver laughed. Anna gave Marcia a look of horror and Marcia could feel a blush rise to her cheeks. *What did I say?*

Justin cleared his throat, a soft smile playing across his lips. "Not all of us Southerners talk like we've just come from tilling the field."

Marcia was embarrassed. "I'm so sorry, I didn't mean to offend you."

Justin put a hand up to stop her. "Please, no offense taken. I was born in New Orleans, but educated abroad. First in boarding schools in Paris, and later in London at the London School of Economics."

Marcia was surprised. "London?"

"Yes. I've actually lived abroad most of my life. My father passed away last year and I had to return home to see to the property."

"Oh, I'm sorry. Was it an illness?"

Justin looked uncomfortable for just a moment. "No, an accident. The plantation was undergoing some renovations and he fell through a hole in one of the cabins, an awful accident."

"I'm sorry." For some reason, Marcia's curiosity had been piqued and she couldn't let the conversation go, even though Anna was silently begging her with her eyes. "And your mother?"

Justin turned his eyes to Anna and then to Marcia. It was obvious by his icy stare that he did not want to talk about his family.

"I apologize if you don't want to talk about this…" Marcia began.

"No, it's all right. My mother has been ill for some time."

"I'm sorry to hear that."

"Thank you. It's quite difficult for us to see her in such a state. She was always such a vibrant and active woman."

Marcia sighed. "I understand. As you know, Anna and I lost our parents when we were quite young."

Justin reached over and took Anna's hand. "Yes, that's probably what drew us together…one of the many reasons."

Anna caressed Justin's hand. "And we're madly in love."

"Yes," Justin said, a soft smile again playing on his lips. He drew Anna to him and they embraced.

Marcia turned to look out onto the street. The night breeze felt cool on her face and she watched as people strolled slowly down the quaint streets. Taking it easy seemed to be the theme of this pleasant city, but something she could not yet put a name to, something uncertain, began to nag at Marcia's heart.

~

They stepped out of the carriage near St. Louis Cathedral in Jackson Square. Marcia stared, mesmerized. All around the old church was scaffolding and makeshift Port-o-lets for construction workers.

"What a beautiful church," Marcia commented. "How long will that scaffold surround it? It does take away from the beauty."

Justin turned to look at the church. "St. Louis Cathedral has been a landmark for over two hundred years. New Orleans has just received a grant to refurbish it, but it'll be a couple of years before we see it restored to its former glory."

Marcia nodded and walked ahead with Anna while Justin paid the carriage driver. Anna leaned in and whispered harshly to Marcia. "Why did you keep going on about his mother? He doesn't like to talk about his parents."

"I was only curious. This man *is* going to be my future brother-in-law. I have a right to know something about the man my sister loves."

Nervously, Anna removed a compact from her purse. With shaky hands she powdered her nose and applied more lipstick, although her lips did not need it.

"Just be polite. That's all I'm asking. I want Justin to like you. It's important to me."

Marcia shook her head. "What's the matter, Anna?"

Anna shrugged her shoulders. "I just want you two to get along."

"We've just met. Give us a chance to get to know one another."

Closing her compact, Anna placed it back inside her purse. She then turned toward Marcia. Anxiety lay in her cool green eyes. "I just want you to be nice to him. He's all I've got. I love him."

Marcia leaned over and took Anna's hand. "What's all this talk about him being all you have? You'll always have me. Take it easy, Anna. I like him, so far, okay? He seems to love you and he's a gentleman. Don't worry, I won't embarrass you."

Anna gave Marcia a half smile and a quick squeeze of her hand and then took Justin's arm as he stepped beside her. He glanced from Anna to Marcia and then taking Anna's hand possessively, attempted a smile. "Shall we go to dinner?"

As they walked slowly down narrow streets to Galatoire's on Bourbon Street, Marcia was again struck by the beauty and quaintness of the French Quarter.

Galatoire's, one of the finest restaurants in New Orleans, immediately impressed Marcia with its charming dining room and chandeliers. The maître d' hurried over to greet Justin and immediately escorted them to the best table in the place, on the first floor, and sent over a bottle of wine, compliments of the house.

As she sat down, Marcia realized that most of the patrons had either nodded or waved at Justin as they made their way to their table. *Justin must be a very powerful man.*

The waiter hurried over and bowed deeply. "Mr. St. Jean, it's nice to see you again. It's been too long."

"Thank you, Henri. How have you been?"

Henri nodded politely. "Fine, thank you. What can I bring for you, Mr. St. Jean?"

Justin smiled at Marcia. "Anna always allows me to order for her. Would you allow me to…?"

"Oh, sure," Marcia said. She closed her menu. "Of course."

Justin nodded and turned to Henri. "The ladies and I shall start with your fried oysters followed by veal in béarnaise sauce." Justin looked over at Marcia, "All right?"

"Fine," Marcia said.

"Then we'll have the seafood stuffed eggplant and the trout almandine…a special treat for our guest."

Henri nodded. "Of course. And perhaps another bottle of wine?"

"Yes, perhaps a bottle of wine for the veal, a burgundy."

"Of course, Mr. St. Jean. For you anything." Henri left to place their order.

"This is a lovely restaurant. There are nice places in Manchester, but not like this," Marcia said, glancing around the restaurant.

"Residents of New Orleans love to eat, that's why we have so many restaurants."

Anna beamed. "I'm so glad you're here, but after dinner, we should let you get a good night's sleep so you'll be ready for a long day of shopping tomorrow."

"Anna, darling, let your sister enjoy her dinner before you start planning out her week."

"It's okay. We're just excited to see each other and it isn't every day that my only sister is engaged to be married," Marcia said, picking up her wine glass. She lifted it in a toast to Anna and Justin. "To Anna and Justin. May your marriage be long and fruitful," she added, winking at Anna, who gave her a kick underneath the table. Marcia turned to wink at Justin and was surprised by the hard look on his face. *Did I say something to insult him?*

But once again, his angry look faded and Justin smiled at Marcia. "Thank you, Marcia, for coming. My Anna would not be happy until she was sure you were coming. In fact, she insisted."

Marcia cringed inwardly a bit at the words *my Anna*, but tried to keep a smile on her face for Anna's sake. "Really?"

Anna nodded. "You're my only family." Tears filled her eyes, and she turned away.

Justin reached over and took her hand. "It's all right, my love. You have me. I'm your family now. And my family, they love you. You're not alone." They shared a passionate kiss.

Marcia's heart ached as she watched them embrace. She was happy for her sister, but sad for herself. *Will I ever find someone to love? Someone who will love me?*

She didn't have long to dwell on her loneliness as the waiter arrived with their fried oysters. Afterwards, their taste buds were captivated with the trout almandine and veal béarnaise, a dish that Marcia had never had before. One taste and she swore that she would have it again. After that, they indulged themselves in tasty crème brûlée.

"I'll never fit into my wedding gown if I keep eating like this," Anna said, leaning back and sipping her café crème.

"What about me? I'm definitely going to have to lose weight before I squeeze into that matron of honor dress."

"Maid," Justin said, not looking up as he stirred his coffee.

"What?" Marcia asked.

Justin looked up and smiled as his hand slowly stirred another packet of sugar into his coffee. "I only meant that one can't be a matron of honor if one is unmarried."

Marcia felt her face flush with embarrassment.

"Justin!" Anna said.

Justin glanced from Marcia to Anna. "I'm sorry, have I said something to offend?"

"Yes, you did," Anna said.

Marcia cleared her throat with a sip of water. *Did he just say what I think he said?*

"It's okay, Anna, no harm done. Justin was just being exact, weren't you, Justin?"

Marcia smiled over at him, but inside she was a bit steamed. She let it go, though. *He's right. I've never been married.*

As Justin took the check and placed his American Express platinum card onto the table, he shook his head and wiped his mouth with his cloth napkin. "Of course. You are still a maiden. That's what I meant. Besides, I'm tired of hearing Anna complain about her waistline. It's always the most beautiful of ladies, ladies who don't have a thing to worry about, who complain."

Anna playfully slapped Justin on the arm. "Oh, you."

Marcia laughed as they stood to leave. *He is a charmer…with a sting.* She made a mental note to stay out of Justin's line of fire.

It was after eleven when Justin and Anna dropped Marcia off on Royal Street. As Marcia made her way inside the foyer into the dimly lit hallway, she felt a cold shiver run along her spine. Turning, she looked behind her, but there was no one there. *I'm imagining things again. I need to get some sleep.* She yawned as she climbed the stairs to the apartment. *Still, this old house is a bit spooky…and where are the other neighbors?*

Marcia suddenly heard a loud thump behind her. Startled she flipped around.

"Hello? Is anyone there?"

Again, there was only silence. Marcia shook her head and hurried to her door, unlocking it and slipping inside. She locked the door behind her and placed her bag on the chair in the living room. She walked into the bedroom and sat on the bed to remove her shoes. As she did so, she saw that some of the dresser drawers were open. *Have I been robbed?*

She stared at the open dresser drawers. It wasn't like her to leave dresser drawers open. She went carefully through her things, but nothing seemed to be missing. *I probably left them open. I must really be tired.* She went into the bathroom to wash her face and brush her teeth. As she slipped out of her clothes and pulled on pajamas, she yawned again. *It's been a long day. I'm going to sleep late.*

Turning off the bathroom light, she walked back into her suddenly chilly bedroom. She hugged herself for warmth and looked around curiously, unable to locate the source of the chill. She checked the air conditioning unit and found that it was turned off. Still shivering, she threw back the duvet and crawled beneath the covers, then leaned over and turned off the table lamp. Despite the blankets covering her, she still shivered. Exhausted, she finally fell asleep anyway.

O-o-o-h...o-o-o-h...o-o-o-h...

She thought at first that the moaning sound was coming from the neighbors next door, but when she sleepily reached over to the wall and banged on it a few times, the moaning did not stop, only grew louder. Fully awake now, she realized that the moaning was coming from *inside* her room.

Marcia sat up in bed, staring anxiously into the darkness, her heart beating rapidly. "Who's there?" Her voice betrayed her fear.

Silence. Marcia blinked, trying to adjust her eyes to the dark. Then, remembering the lamp beside the bed, she reached over and switched it on.

With the blankets drawn up to her chin, Marcia examined the room. She was alone. *It sounds like a woman's moan.* "Hello?"

Still no answer, just the gentle ticking of the clock on the bedside table. *Must be my imagination.* She shrugged, switched off the light and lay back down, closing her eyes. *A bad nightmare I suppose.*

Just as she hovered at the edge of sleep, Marcia was again startled by the persistent moaning sound. She sat up in the darkness, her heart racing.

O-o-o-h...o-o-o-h...o-o-o-h...

Where's that noise coming from? She flicked on the lamp, looked around the room, then threw back the covers, and got up. She walked over to the wall and flicked on the overhead light. She was alone. Her heartbeat had just begun to slow down when a sudden chill across the back of her neck rooted her feet to the floor. She swallowed, her breath catching at the back of her throat and listened. All she heard was the beating of her own heart and the ticking of the clock on the bedside table. Slowly, keeping her back to the wall, she sidestepped until she reached the bathroom and flicked on that light.

What's going on? As if in answer to her question, the soft sounds of a woman in pain again came to her ears. There was no doubt. It was coming from *inside* her room. She whirled around, her fear so intense it almost suffocated her. *Take it easy…it's nothing…nothing.* All at once, the moaning seemed to fill the room and then died away. Her eyes wide with fright, Marcia waited for someone or something to appear, yet she remained alone in the room, bracing herself against the doorframe.

"What is it? Who's there?"

There was no reply.

"Who's there?"

No answer.

"Anyone there?"

Silence.

Just as she was about to relax, a moan again echoed in the room. *O-o-o-h…o-o-o-h…o-o-o-h…*

With labored breath, she called out. "What do you want?"

A soft voice, barely audible, as if gathering courage, finally answered. "Sam. Help me find my Sam."

"Sam? Who's Sam? Who are you? Where are you?" Marcia asked, searching the room for the mysterious person behind the voice.

"Sam. Help me…please. Help me…find him."

A moment later, the coldness of the room dissipated and Marcia sensed that she was alone.

CHAPTER FOUR

Marcia spent the rest of the night tossing and turning. Not until dawn did sleep return and shortly after, the street noises awakened her. Marcia sat up in bed and looked around the room cautiously. She was alone. Soft sunlight from the crack between the French doors drifted into the room. She glanced over at the bedside clock and saw that it was a little past seven in the morning. She yawned and stretched her arms over her head, threw back the bedclothes, got up, and pulling on her robe, made her way to the French doors. Throwing them open, she walked out onto the balcony to take in the street below. Street cleaners were sweeping the walk and then washing it down with water. Across the street, she could see a woman opening her green shutters and placing her flowerpots on the ledge. Smiling to herself, Marcia then walked back in the room.

Upon entering the room, she glanced around. She breathed out a sigh of relief at discovering that she was indeed still alone in the room. *Bad nightmare…too much rich food.*

She walked over to the bathroom and flicked on the light. *Was it all a bad dream? Pretty vivid dream.* She shook her head and laughed at herself in the bathroom mirror as she got undressed. *That's what I get for eating so late…I think one week in New Orleans is going to blast my diet from memory.* She decided to take a quick shower and then have a nice long walk around the neighborhood before she called her sister to meet for breakfast.

As she stepped into the shower, her thoughts were again on her sister and her future brother-in-law. Although Justin seemed to be a charming fellow, there was just something disquieting about him. Anna had always been an independent girl who never liked being told what to do, not even by their parents. Though they had been close growing up,

Anna had at first resented Marcia when she became her legal guardian. There had been arguments and tears, but through it all, the women had always managed to patch things up. As she worked the shampoo through her hair, Marcia shook her head. *I don't know. Maybe it's just paranoia. Thinking no one is good enough for Anna.* Yet she remembered how Justin had tried to control the conversation throughout dinner and how he'd held onto Anna's hand so possessively. As Marcia rinsed off the shampoo and combed in conditioner, she hoped that she was just being overcautious. She hadn't seen Anna so happy in a long time and she wanted to see her sister settled and content, for once in her life. Their parents' deaths had been difficult for her, but even more so for Anna as she was so young. Even though Marcia had tried to be both a mother and father to her younger sister, she knew that she could never make up for their parents not being there. A thought occurred to her. Perhaps that was why Anna had fallen for an older man. Maybe she was looking for stability, maybe even a father figure. *Justin is certainly that.*

After rinsing off the conditioner, she scrubbed body soap all over her body, shaved her legs and then rinsing one more time, turned off the water and stepped out of the shower. She grabbed a big fluffy towel and began to dry herself. Maybe it was all for the best. After all, no one was perfect and even if Justin were a bit bossy and arrogant, he would take good care of Anna, Marcia was sure of that. And, it was what Anna wanted. Marcia got into a terrycloth robe and walked out of the bathroom. She began to shiver as soon as she stepped into the bedroom. She hurried over to the French doors, shut and latched them tightly, and wrapped the robe tighter around her body. It was then that she noticed that once again, the dresser drawers sat open. *I sure am getting absentminded. All the hard work these past few weeks must be catching up with me.* She walked over and pulled out a matching bra and panties and slipped into them. She then threw on a pair of slacks and T-shirt and walked over to the bed to pull on her sandals before walking back into the bathroom to finish preparing for the day.

When she stepped out into the hallway and locked her door, she heard piano music coming from across the hall, followed by a deep and beautiful male voice singing "You Look Wonderful Tonight." She paused to listen at the door, feeling foolish for invading her neighbor's privacy, but unable to stop herself. *Whoever he is, he should be on stage.* When the song was finished, the man began another song. Marcia stood rooted, mesmerized by the emotion in the singer's voice. When the song finished, she clapped, not able to stop herself. Suddenly Marcia heard footsteps coming toward the door and stepped away just as it was opened.

There in the doorway stood the most handsome man Marcia had ever laid eyes on. His tall, lean frame and muscled arms were complemented by a deep mocha chocolate complexion and hazel eyes. His salt and pepper hair was cut close to his scalp and Marcia wanted to run her hands over his finely-shaped head. But the man's stern look stopped her.

"Can I help you?" he asked.

"I'm sorry. I—"

"Did you want something, ma'am? Something wrong with the apartment?"

It was then that Marcia recalled Justin telling her that the landlord, Walter Dufrane, lived across the hall. *Can this be the landlord? This handsome man with such a beautiful voice?*

"No, I…sorry, Mr. Dufrane…I was just listening…"

"I'll thank you to respect my privacy, ma'am, while you're here. Have a nice day, ma'am." With that, the man shut the door and locked it.

Marcia was shocked by the man's rudeness. *Why was he so rude? I was just listening.* She shook her head and as she made her way down the staircase, she told herself to stay away from Walter Dufrane.

As soon as she stepped outside into the warm sunshine, Marcia was once again glad that she had come to New Orleans. She made her way slowly down Royal Street, past the Dauphine Orleans Hotel with its pink and white flags. Deciding to continue her walk before calling Anna, she made a left onto Toulouse Street and then a right onto Bourbon Street. As she strolled past the various bars and lounges, nudie shops and Triple X variety stores, she was shocked. In pictures of New Orleans, Bourbon Street looked elegant and demure. But the real thing was very different. She glanced down at scattered paper beer cups, cigarette butts, and patches of vomit. *Mardi Gras must be a real party in this town. If the streets look like this on a typical Thursday night, I can't imagine what they look like after a Mardi Gras celebration.* She wondered how the local residents could stand to see so many people milling around their beautiful French Quarter, drunk and half naked.

As Marcia turned back onto Toulouse, she again thought of the incident last night. Goose bumps began to spread across her arms and neck as she thought of the voice begging her to help find "her Sam." Had it been a nightmare? If not, then who was this Sam and why was someone looking for him?

Over a breakfast of beignets and coffee at the world famous Café Du Monde, Marcia recounted her nightmare for Justin and Anna.

"I don't know," she finished. "I think it was just a dream, but when I woke up this morning, I was so afraid. It seemed real." Marcia stirred the milk in her coffee.

"That's rather hard to believe," Justin said.

"I know. After I had a chance to get my bearings, I chided myself for thinking that it was real for even a moment. It must have been all that delicious New Orleans food last night."

"Yes. I'm quite sure that's what it was. After all, you don't really believe in ghosts, do you?" Justin raised one eyebrow inquisitively.

Marcia looked over at Justin, surprised by his question. "Well, yes and no."

"Really?" Justin said as he sat up straighter in his chair. "I wouldn't have taken you for a believer in the supernatural."

"I don't know if I'm a believer, but I would say that until someone absolutely disproves the idea of ghosts, then I'll be open to the possibility that they might exist. If you'd heard what I heard last night, you might change your opinion."

Justin laughed a deep throaty laugh that irked Marcia.

"There's no need to laugh. I'm not some child who's scared of the boogey man. What I heard last night, at least what I believe I heard, was real, at least at that moment."

"I apologize if I've come off flippant. That was certainly not my intention," Justin offered.

Anna laughed, trying to ease the tension. "Oh, all this talk of ghosts! Justin, would you mind getting me another coffee?"

Marcia took a bite of her beignet and stared over at her sister, puzzled. Her sister was not a Southern belle, but she was certainly doing her best imitation.

"Of course, my dear." As Justin did not see a waitress, he stood, kissed her hand and walked inside the café to order the coffee.

"I'm sorry," Marcia said immediately.

Anna patted her hand. "What are you sorry about? I would have been scared to death if it had been me."

Marcia nodded and taking another bite of the beignet, chewed thoughtfully.

"You know, there's always been talk that that place is haunted. Justin just laughs at the very idea, but I've often wondered. I mean, when he suggested you stay there, I was excited for you because it's so opulent, but it just makes me uncomfortable to be there. I guess I should have insisted that Justin put you up in a hotel."

"Why does it make you uncomfortable?"

Anna shook her head. "Don't know, really. Just gives me the creeps is all. Can't explain why."

Marcia reached over and took hold of Anna's hand. "Anna, don't worry. I had a bad nightmare. Now, I want you to stop worrying about me. I love New Orleans so far and besides, this is your week. The apartment is wonderful. Now, please, I shouldn't have even brought up my stupid nightmare. It was nothing. Put it out of your mind, okay?"

Anna immediately brightened up. "All right."

Marcia smiled at her younger sister. "Now let's talk about the wedding. What are the plans today? Shopping?"

"Definitely, but later this afternoon, I have to meet up with Justin. I have a doctor's appointment."

"Doctor's? Is everything all right?"

"Sure it is. Justin wants me to get checked out by the doctor."

"Checked out? For what?"

"To see if everything's all right with me."

Marcia was alarmed. "All right? Why wouldn't it be? Is there something you're not telling—"

"Calm down," Anna replied. "Justin wants to make sure I can have children before we get married."

"Oh?"

"I know what you're thinking, but don't. Tiffany, Justin's wife who died, couldn't have kids and Justin has always wanted children."

"But you're not thinking of having children right away, are you?"

When Anna hesitated before answering, Marcia continued. "It's too soon. What's all the rush? Are you ready to have kids?"

"I think so."

Marcia shook her head. "Children are a big responsibility."

Anna glared at her. "How would you know? You don't have any." Then she immediately leaned over and grabbed her hand. "I'm sorry, Marcia. You know I didn't mean that."

Marcia pushed away the sting from Anna's words and continued. "I raised you by myself after Mom and Dad died. You're not just my sister; you're like my own child. I just don't want you to rush into something you're not ready for."

"I know you're worried, but don't be. Justin assures me that I'll have plenty of help. Nannies, maids, whatever I need."

"But that's not the way to raise children. You need to raise them if you have them, not someone else."

"I will." She glanced up. "Justin's coming, so enough of this, all right?"

Justin sat down with the coffees. "What arrangements have you ladies made so far?"

"Oh, just talking is all," Anna said, giving Marcia a look.

Marcia sipped her coffee and glanced around the packed café. There were local residents sitting on the outside patio, reading the *Times Picayune* and tourists wearing shorts and T-shirts standing in line to buy cups and other Café Du Monde memorabilia. Justin wrapped his arm around Anna's shoulders and smiled at Marcia. Marcia didn't like the way that he held onto Anna so possessively.

"I'll let you and Anna do some shopping for the wedding. Later, I'd like to take you both to dinner at G.W. Fins. They have some of the best seafood in New Orleans. Would that suit you?"

"That's fine by us."

"When exactly is the wedding? I've been told in a week, but…"

"Saturday next," Justin replied, adding sugar to his coffee.

Marcia shook her head. "Doesn't give us much time to buy dresses and plan."

"No need to worry about the planning. I've taken care of all the arrangements."

Anna looked at Justin in surprise. "You have? You didn't tell me that."

Justin gently patted Anna's hand. "I knew you had a lot on your mind, my darling, what with your dress and your sister arriving. I didn't want you to have to worry about planning the reception, flowers."

"But Justin, it's my wedding, too. I mean, I don't even know where we're going to get married."

"St. Mary's Church. The reception will be at the Ritz Carlton. There will be a cocktail reception in the Grand Hall followed by a sit down dinner of beef bourguignon."

"But…?"

"You'll love it darling. It's French, quite delectable. For the cake, I've taken the liberty of ordering a three tier chocolate mousse with a chocolate foundation."

Anna looked disappointed. "I wanted to order the cake. I was hoping to do that today with Marcia. It was going to be a treat to try all the different flavors."

He picked up her hand and kissed it delicately. "Maybe it was best that I ordered it then. I don't want you getting heavy before our blessed day."

Marcia tried not to cringe when she heard that.

"But my sister came out early, a whole week off from her business to help with the wedding plans and now you say you've taken care of everything. What does that leave me to do?"

"Like I said, Anna, my darling, you've enough to worry about with the wedding dress and looking beautiful on our big day." He touched her face with his fingertips. "Don't worry. You'll be quite satisfied."

"I don't know…"

Marcia looked from Anna to Justin, but kept quiet. She knew her sister wanted to have a say in what kind of wedding she had, but it seemed that Justin liked to have control of everything. Anna was visibly upset, but when she looked at Marcia, she smiled, masking her disappointment. Justin sat back and finished his coffee, all the while clasping Anna's hand possessively in his.

"It's fine, Anna," Marcia lied. "I'm glad I came early. It's a lot of work finding a dress and getting it all ready in one week! And then there's my dress, and exploring New Orleans. We've got tons to do. After all, I get to see where you live and work and meet all your friends."

She could see from the corner of her eye that Justin was displeased by this. But Anna perked up.

"Yeah. I can show you my old apartment and then we can stop by and have a drink at the Louis Armstrong. My co-workers are dying to meet you."

"Great," Marcia said. "It's a date."

"Are you sure you want to show your sister that decrepit place you once called a home? Perhaps it's best…"

"It's not so bad. And I still live there, technically. I want Marcia to see my old place and to meet my friends."

Justin nodded and smiled, but she could see that Justin St. Jean, whose hand still possessively clasped Anna's, didn't like not having his way.

Marcia and Anna spent most of the early morning shopping in the small boutiques and shops around New Orleans. It was hard going, but Marcia trudged on, from one shop to the next, because Anna was so excited and wanted to try on every dress. They stopped in the late morning to have tea at the Sheraton in the Garden District and then took the St. Charles streetcar back to the French Quarter. At Riverwalk, an inside mall, they looked through the bridal boutique and antique jewelry shops before stopping for a quick break at the Café Du Monde again. Marcia couldn't get enough of their beignets. After their snack, they went outside by the water and saw a Carnival cruise ship leaving port. Anna waved at the people aboard and then came to sit down on a bench next to Marcia.

"Did you like any of the dresses we saw today?" Marcia asked. Her feet were aching and she slid her sandals off so she could rub them.

"The one at Saks was beautiful, but I want Justin to see it first before I buy it."

"Really? Isn't that bad luck?"

Anna laughed and shook her head. "No. It's just bad luck on the day of the wedding. Besides, Justin is so picky. The dress has to be elegant and tasteful."

"But what about you? What kind of dress do *you* want to wear? You're going to be the one wearing the dress."

"I know, but Justin's paying for it."

"So what? It's obvious he makes more money than you do."

"Still, he makes me so happy and he asks very little of me. I can let him have his way once in a while."

"Or most of the time."

Anna turned to her. "What do you mean?"

"Weren't you just a little bit disappointed this morning at having been left out of planning your own wedding?"

Anna turned away. The ship sounded its horn. "I didn't think you'd noticed."

"Of course I did. Listen, Anna, how well do you know Justin?"

"I told you, two months. Why does that matter when two people are in love?"

Marcia raised an eyebrow, but Anna held up her hand to stop her from speaking. "I know what you're going to say. But I love Justin and want to spend the rest of my life with him. He loves me, too."

"But you can still be engaged and postpone the wedding for, say, this time next year. A one year engagement is very common. It gives both the bride and groom time to seriously think about being married."

"No. We've already talked about that. Justin wants to get married right away."

Marcia put her hand on Anna's shoulder. "I've never seen you so nervous."

"And happy."

Marcia nodded her head. "True, but…"

Anna pulled away. "I want to make him happy. Now, I know you're my older sister and all, but I'm a grown woman now. I can take care of myself. I'm marrying Justin. He's the best thing that ever happened to me."

"And you're the best thing that ever happened to him."

"No, I'm not. Justin is rich and handsome, and he could get anyone he wants—"

"He wants you."

"I know and I'm going to do everything I can to keep him."

Marcia shook her head. "What's happened to my independent and confident sister? You act as if Justin St. Jean is your only chance at real happiness."

"He is. I mean, I know I'll be happy with him. 'Time doesn't matter,' Justin always says. When you find the one you want to spend the rest of your life with, it doesn't matter how long you know each other."

"Are those your words or Justin's?"

"Mine."

"What about after the wedding?"

"What do you mean?"

"Are you going to be making any of the decisions after you're married? It seems Justin likes to run things."

Anna shrugged. "He doesn't mean to be bossy. He's just used to being in control. I don't mind."

Marcia wasn't convinced, but she was determined not to spoil their day. She put her sandals back on. "Have you decided where you're going on your honeymoon?"

Anna shook her head. "I don't know. Justin says it's a surprise."

"That's mighty considerate of him."

"I was hoping to have more of a say about the reception hall, but you heard him. Justin says it's best if I just stick to the dress."

"What about an engagement party?"

"There's going to be a get-together at his parents' estate on Saturday night. You'll get to meet Justin's mom and all his family and they'll finally get to meet you."

"Wonderful to be with such an organized man, isn't it?"

Anna nodded. "He doesn't like me to worry too much."

Marcia turned to look at Anna. "He is considerate when he's ordering you around."

"Marcia…"

"You know, I'm wondering when you're going to bring up your singing. You haven't yet."

Anna turned away from her. "It's over."

"What's over?"

"Singing. I've given it up. It was a stupid, childish dream."

"What do you mean? It's all you've lived for since you were a kid. You've got real talent—"

"No I don't! If I did, I would have made it by now."

"What are you talking about? You've barely tried."

"How would you know? I've been through a lot. I've gone to practically all the clubs in this town and begged them to give me a chance, but the only way I'll get a chance to sing is if I sleep with the owner."

"Anna," Marcia said as she reached for her, "I had no idea. Why didn't you tell me how hard it's been?"

Anna pulled away. "You never asked how that part of my life was going."

"I'm sorry. I just assumed things were okay. I was worried that you weren't making ends meet…," Marcia began.

"It's been so hard," Anna said, cutting her off. "If you don't have money or a famous name, it's impossible. I'm pretty enough and I know I can sing, but it's tough just to get an audition. I begged my boss for two years to give me a chance, but he refused. 'Louis Armstrong never takes a chance on no-name performers,' he told me. 'Try out Amateur Night.'"

"So? Why don't you?"

Anna gave her a cold look. "Amateur Night is a joke. It's for drunken frat boys and old men who stand up there and pretend to sing."

"Why didn't you talk to me about all this before? Whenever we talked, you said things were going well."

"After I dropped out of school, all you ever asked me was whether I needed money and if I still had a job. It was like all you cared about was whether I was making the rent and what I had for dinner."

"I worry about you, Anna. I'm sorry if I didn't ask about your singing…I know how important it is to you."

"Yeah, it's all for the best. I've been here two years and nothing's happened. It wasn't meant to be."

"How can you give up so easily? I didn't raise you to be a quitter."

Anna immediately straightened up. "I'm not. I've tried. I'm getting too old and—"

"Wait a minute. What do you mean 'too old'? You're only twenty-five."

"You've got to be young to succeed in the music industry."

"When did twenty-five stop being young? And what's this business about the 'music industry'? I know you'd love a music contract, but you've got to work to get there. Do you think it was easy for me to get to where I am? I had to work and put myself through school and worry about you. And there were jerks in New York just like in New Orleans. Guys who want a piece of you before they give you a shot. But you know what I did?"

"What?"

"I ignored them. It was always my dream to be a designer. And look at me now. I have my own company and I'm doing well for myself. If I'd let a couple of jerks dissuade me, I might have ended up being—"

"A waitress, like me."

"Please Anna, stop feeling sorry for yourself. It's ridiculous. So what if you haven't made it yet. It's only been two years. You said you've been to most of the clubs in New Orleans, but not all of them. Knock on every door and then at least you can say to yourself that you tried everything. You can't wait for opportunity to come knocking on your door. You've got to find opportunity. Look at me, a black woman with my own company, living in my own home in Vermont. I went after that myself. Nobody ever handed me anything on a silver platter."

"I'm not asking for it to be handed to me on a silver platter. It just didn't happen, okay?"

"All right, Anna, but you have a beautiful voice. Don't waste your God-given talent."

"It won't do any good. All the clubs in New Orleans want names and exposure—"

"So tell them you can't have exposure if no one gives you a chance to get on stage. Try all your options before just giving up. Maybe you should think about moving away from here. Move to a city where there are a lot more clubs, like New York or Atlanta or Los Angeles."

"I can't move. I'm getting married."

"So? Postpone the wedding or take Justin with you. He'll understand if he loves you. It's your dream to be a singer. Don't give up so easily, Anna."

"Not anymore it isn't. It's too late. I've already given up. I'm marrying Justin and that's that."

Marcia suddenly got a sick feeling in her stomach. "Please don't tell me that you're marrying Justin just so you can have an excuse not to follow your dreams. Please tell me that's not what I'm hearing."

"I'm marrying Justin because I love him. Besides, Justin would never move to another city. His family is here."

"Sure he would. Have you asked him? He sounds like a well-traveled man to me. He's lived in Europe, and I'm sure he wouldn't mind moving to New York so his future wife could pursue her dream, singing."

Anna stood, shaking her head. "No, he doesn't want a wife that works. He wants to settle down and have children."

"Is that what you want?"

"It is now. Please, Marcia, let's drop this. I've already made up my mind. Next Saturday I am going to become Mrs. Justin St. Jean. Life is going to be much easier that way. I'll never have to worry again, and you'll never have to worry about me. All right?"

"Life's not going to be any easier as Mrs. Justin St. Jean. He's an important man and you'll be the wife of an important man. There will be parties, social events and functions, where you'll have to be cheery and entertain people, even when you're exhausted. And you want to have kids right away on top of that. Doesn't sound like an easy life to me."

"Marcia, I said let's drop it. I've made up my mind. Did you come here to support me or to be negative?"

Marcia stood, stretching her legs. "Fine, whatever you want. There's just nothing wrong with waiting on this wedding. If Justin really loves

A LOVER'S LEGACY

you, he'll understand. These things get postponed all the time. Don't feel just because he's already made arrange—"

"I told you already. Justin doesn't want to wait. You sound like a broken record."

"Aren't you worth waiting for?"

"You've waited, and look at you now. You're still alone. I don't want to end up like you."

The words cut Marcia like a knife. Anna turned and her face fell when she saw how she had hurt Marcia. "I'm sorry, Marcia, I didn't mean—"

"You're right," Marcia said. "I know I'll find the right person for me, but I'm willing to wait. I'm not going to marry someone because I'm afraid of living my life."

"I'm not afraid. Let's stop all this talk. Let's go get something to eat."

Marcia dropped the conversation for Anna's sake, but that feeling of worry filled her heart again. Anna seemed set on marrying Justin, but Marcia still wasn't sure Anna knew what she was getting herself into.

After a leisurely lunch at the famous Mr. B's Bistro, they went over to Anna's apartment on Toulouse Street. The outside was a bit ramshackled, but the colors, green, pink and white shutters alongside a balcony, gave the building a quaint French Quarter look. Marcia climbed up a pair of rickety steps to a small apartment, minimally decorated, on the second floor. The hallway smelled musty and needed a good moping.

Anna turned to look at her and laughed when she saw Marcia's disapproving expression.

"I know what you're thinking. But the homes in the Quarter are all old and you can't tear them down to rebuild. Most of them have that musty smell, too."

"How much rent do you pay a month?"

"$1,200."

"$1,200! Are you kidding me?"

"Don't worry, that's to share. I pay $600."

"I'm suddenly happy you're getting married and getting out of here."

"Thanks," Anna said as she opened the door. Marcia stepped inside after Anna and was shocked at what she saw. The apartment was in a general state of disrepair, from broken floorboards to mismatched tiles in the cluttered kitchen. There was a stack of unwashed dishes in the sink and she could smell garbage.

"Anna, how can you live like this?" Marcia asked as she held her nose.

"I know, it's awful. But I haven't been here for a week and my room-mate Natasha wouldn't get the medal of the year award for cleanliness. I'll open the window and take out the garbage. My room's in the back. Go on in and I'll be there in a minute."

Marcia walked past a small living room with an old sofa and chipped coffee table, which was at that moment covered with newspaper articles.

"What does your roommate do?"

"She's still in school. She wants to be a journalist."

"You'd think she could learn to tidy up a bit now and again." Marcia found her way along the dark hallway to a small room in the back. When she opened the door, she thought at first it was a closet. "Is this your room?" she called.

"Yes, Natasha's is on the right."

Marcia opened the room on the right and practically recoiled from the smell of soiled clothes. There were clothes piled high on the floor and bed and there were empty chocolate wrappers strewn about the room. Natasha never winning any awards for cleanliness was an understatement. The room was a hazard zone. She shut the door quickly.

Marcia walked into Anna's room which was no bigger than 10 x 10. There was a small door that led out onto the balcony she had seen from outside. The room itself was clean and tidy, and she recognized Anna's vanity and bed. There were boxes neatly stacked along the wall. "At least your room is decent, even though it's tiny."

Anna appeared at the door with glasses of lemonade. She handed one to Marcia and then walked over to a phone by her bedside table. "It's not that small."

Marcia sat down on the bed and took a sip of the lemonade. "Honey, the last time I saw such a small room was in New York City when I was going to Parsons. You pay a lot for what you get."

"I don't have to worry about that anymore because I'm going to be living with Justin and his family. His home is huge."

"They don't mind you living there?"

"Nope," Anna said, dialing the phone. "His mother adores me. I even have my own room in the same wing as Justin."

"*Wing?* How big is this house?"

"Real big. You'll see on Saturday. She said that once we're married, Justin and I can have one whole wing to ourselves. That means two bedrooms, a living room, dining room and kitchen."

"Wow, sounds great, but don't you and Justin want your own place? I mean, it's not very private, is it, to live with the in-laws?"

"We'll have some privacy. His brother lives there with his family and we hardly ever see them, except at meal times. Besides, Justin wants to live there so he can be close to his mother. She's not well."

"I heard, but what do *you* want?"

"It doesn't matter to me. I just want to get out of here."

"It's gonna be hard to get to work, isn't it?"

But Anna didn't answer her question. She was on the phone talking to someone. Marcia sipped her lemonade and waited for her sister to finish.

"Okay, see you tonight then. I know it will, but it's been great."

Anna hung up the phone and walked over to her closet and grabbed a shirt to change into.

"Who were you calling?"

"The Louis Armstrong. Sheryl suggested we stop by tonight. They've got a great band lined up for this evening."

"Fine by me, but will Justin go for the idea? He seemed uncomfortable this afternoon."

"Justin doesn't like the Louis Armstrong. He thinks there are too many men there, ogling me and the other waitresses. He worries about me working there late."

"There's nothing wrong with a man worrying about his fiancée."

"Nope." Anna smiled at Marcia as she buttoned her shirt. "Packing will have to wait for tomorrow. I'm gonna miss this room, though. The one great thing was that balcony."

Marcia walked over to the door and stepped out onto the balcony. It overlooked Toulouse Street. "You're right," she called, "it's great out here." Anna joined her.

"It's your last week as a single woman. How do you feel?"

Anna laughed. "Fine. I always hated the dating scene, all that talk and nonsense."

Marcia thought of all of Anna's boyfriends over the years, so many names and faces melding into one. Beautiful Anna had never been alone for long. The old Anna, self-confident, the life of the party, was nothing like the new Anna, a sophisticated but somewhat distant woman. She wondered if it was all an act to keep Justin. She wanted to really talk to Anna, but instead, she smiled and said, "I don't much like the dating scene myself."

"I'm sorry about what I said before. I'm sure you'll find the right guy soon. And then we'll both be married women."

Anna started to go inside, but Marcia grabbed her arm, stopping her. "Maybe you should ask your manager...uh...what's his name?"

"Ed."

"Right, Ed, when the next Amateur Night is."

"I told you no."

"Why?"

"It's a joke."

"An opportunity is an opportunity. Even if no talent agents come to Amateur Night, at least you can get on stage and practice singing in front of a crowd. Maybe, just maybe, one of these days someone who has connections will see you and then you'll be on your way."

"That's a big maybe. Besides, that never happens, except in the movies. 'Small town girl makes it big.' Or 'Small town girl discovered in jazz joint swilling gin and beer.'"

"Oh Anna, you've got an excuse for everything. You say that I'm negative, but you should hear yourself."

"I'm better than the idiots on Amateur Night. It's for weirdos who can't sing a note. No one takes it seriously. I told you."

"But…"

"No, it's all right, Marcia. I just never made it. Let me move on with my life."

Marcia shrugged her shoulders and went back inside. Anna followed her. "Don't worry, I know what I'm doing, all right?"

"Whatever you want."

Marcia returned to the apartment to rest and shower before dinner. She changed into pajamas and collapsed on top of the canopied bed. She shut her eyes, but couldn't fall asleep. She was worried about Anna and wasn't quite sure her little sister knew what a huge responsibility marriage was. She was worried that after her sister became Mrs. Justin St. Jean, her music dreams would be out the door forever, replaced by the desire to have children.

Not like you would know what she's going through. Marcia had never met Mr. Right, if there was such a thing, but deep down, she had concerns about Justin already. From what she knew of the man, what she'd gathered in the last two days, he was extremely charming and well-to-do, educated and well-spoken, but also demanding and very controlling. She didn't like the way he was constantly monitoring her sister's actions and words. Her sister had never before been one to back down, not from anything, especially during a conversation. But Anna seemed mesmerized by Justin, willing to dress the way he wanted her to, live where he wanted and to do as he said. Marcia turned over onto her side and thought of their parents. *What would Mom and Dad have thought of Justin?* They would have been shocked by the age difference, and, perhaps, surprised a bit by such a quick marriage. Although Anna had assured her that marrying Justin was what she wanted, Marcia was still a bit uneasy. Was Anna lying to her? Was there another reason?

Yet she had seen the way Anna doted on Justin, hung on his every word. No, Anna Watkins was in love, deeply in love, and Justin did seem to care for her sister. By next week, Anna would be Mrs. St. Jean and she would be on a plane back to Vermont. There wasn't much time to get to know Justin St. Jean. But she was determined to find out as much as she could about him before her sister made a decision she might live to regret. She hoped that it would all work out. She hated to see her sister get hurt.

She didn't realize she'd dozed off until she felt herself shivering and got underneath the covers. Suddenly her eyes flew open and she sat up in bed. The dresser drawers were once again open and Marcia was certain there was somebody, *something* in the room.

"Hello? Anyone there?"

The room was so cold, she could see her breath in the air as she breathed in and out, listening.

"Hello?"

Suddenly she heard moaning, and then a voice, soft and definitely female. "Sam…help me…find Sam."

"Who are you?" Marcia asked.

"Sam…help me find Sam."

"Who are you?"

"Sam…please."

"Who are you? Where are you? Show yourself," Marcia said, gripping the blanket in her hand.

"Sam…"

Just as before, silence fell once again and the room temperature returned to normal. Marcia remained in bed, still trembling from fear, tightly clutching the blanket.

CHAPTER FIVE

Dressed in her pajamas and a robe she'd hastily thrown on, Marcia banged on the door across the hall. Scared out of her wits by the voice, she had decided to seek comfort from the only other person in the place, the landlord, Walter Dufrane. She again pounded on the door.

"Mr. Dufrane? Please answer the door if you're home. This is an emergency!"

There was no response, so Marcia continued pounding on the door. Suddenly the door was opened.

"May I help you?" he asked hesitantly.

Marcia had trouble finding her voice. She smiled nervously, aware of the handsome man's eyes on her. He was wearing a white T-shirt and jeans which accentuated his athletic frame. *God, he is gorgeous. Take a breath…easy. Don't say something stupid.* "Mr. Dufrane?"

"Yes?"

"I'm Marcia Watkins."

"Yes?"

"I'm staying across the ha—"

"Yes, I know. Mr. St. Jean's guest. Is there something I can do for you?"

Marcia was again taken aback by his bluntness, but as she glanced behind her at the apartment, she was certain she did not want to return there alone.

"I—"

"Yes?" he asked impatiently.

"I was wondering if you could come with me back to my apartment."

"Why?"

"I—" She didn't know how to phrase the next sentence without coming off as a crazy fool, but she didn't know any other way to describe what she had heard and felt.

"I—something."

"Something? What?" He looked at her with one eyebrow raised.

"Something…" She felt her face grow warm, and her hands began to sweat. Standing there in her robe and pajamas in front of the attractive man had her quivering with nervousness.

"There's something in my room," she finally said.

He was curious now. "Something? Oh, no. Don't tell me you saw a mouse. I've just had this place inspected and—"

"No, it wasn't a mouse."

"A cockroach then? They're pests, any time of year. Sorry about that. Not a nice thing to see. I'd better call the exterminator." He turned to go back inside, but Marcia's words stopped him.

"No!"

He turned back to face her. "Excuse me?"

"No," Marcia said as calmly as she could. "I didn't see a mouse, or any cockroaches. I—if you would just come with me, I can better explain."

He hesitated a moment before opening the door wider and stepping out into the hall. He shut his door and locked it with one of the keys on his heavy keychain. Looking at him standing there, in full view, Marcia felt her breath catch at the back of her throat. Walter Dufrane was indeed the single most handsome man she had ever seen. He caught her looking at him and turned away, shoving his hands into his pocket.

"I'm ready when you are," he said.

"Thank you, Mr. Dufrane."

"Mr. Dufrane was my father. Call me Walter."

She stuck out her hand. "I'm Marcia."

Walter again hesitated before quickly shaking her hand. "Lead the way, ma'am."

Walter waited while Marcia unlocked the door. She stepped inside first, looking anxiously around. Walter walked in slowly behind her. The room was as she had left it, but the cold chill was gone.

"So it wasn't a mouse or a cockroach?"

"No, I—felt something—a cold chill in the air. But it's gone now," she said.

"Hmmm…must be the air conditioning unit," Walter said as he walked over to it. "Sorry about that. I'll turn it down." He walked over to the unit and twisted the knob. Marcia found herself admiring his strong arms and lean frame again.

"There, that ought to do it."

"Thank you," she said as she walked over to the chair and sat down, adjusting the robe's belt around her waist. She felt self-conscious at being so undressed in front of him, but she was glad she wasn't alone in the room. Her mind was racing, trying to think of something to say to him to keep him in the room with her. But the only thing she could think about was the way his muscular arms looked in his shirt and how a trickle of perspiration was making its way down his brow toward his finely shaped nose. She wanted to wipe it away, but shook her head instead, chiding herself for having thoughts about him at such a time.

"Anything else you need, Mrs. Watkins?"

"It's Ms. Watkins. Please, call me Marcia."

"All right, anything else you need, ma'am?"

"Uh—no."

Walter nodded and started to walk to the door. Marcia stood quickly.

"Wait!"

Walter turned to look at her. "Yes…?"

She shook her head and sank back down in the chair. "I feel so silly saying this. I'm an educated woman, for God's sake." Marcia looked over at Walter who was taking her in with a serious look on his face. "I feel like such a fool."

"Why don't you let me be the judge of that."

"You promise not to laugh?"

Walter seemed surprised by her question. "Why would I laugh? Are you going to tell a joke?"

"No, it's just—" Marcia took a deep breath. "Last night when I arrived, I felt this strange…strange…"

"What?"

"Presence. That's exactly what it was. A strange presence in the room. Then when I got out of the shower, all my dresser drawers were open and I could have sworn I'd shut them all. Then when I got back from dinner, the room was freezing, but I had turned the air conditioning off. Then…"

"Go on." He leaned up against the wall.

"Last night, I was awoken by—by a voice."

"A voice?"

"Yes."

"What kind of voice?"

"Female. Definitely female. At first I thought it was coming from the hallway or perhaps a room nearby."

"But it wasn't?"

"No." Marcia shook her head. "It was coming from inside my room. I thought at first that I must be dreaming, or that I was so tired I was hallucinating, but I wasn't. I heard it again."

"When?"

"Right before I knocked on your door. I was taking a nap and the voice…I heard it."

"What did the voice say?"

"At first it said nothing, just moaned, but then it asked for help. 'Help me find Sam,' it said."

Walter crossed his arms and took a look around the room. "Ah, I see. That's not strange at all."

"It's not?"

"No. You see, ma'am…"

"Please, don't call me ma'am."

Walter hesitated for a moment and then nodded his head. "All right, Marcia. You see, lots of folks have had 'experiences' while staying here at the LaLaurie Mansion."

"Really, why?"

Walter turned to her. "Because it's haunted, of course."

The matter of fact way that Walter spoke those words made chills crawl up and down Marcia's spine. "Haunted?"

"Yes. Been haunted going on now a hundred and fifty years or so."

Marcia sank back against the cushion of the chair. "I thought...I'm not surprised, I guess."

"Listen, what you experienced isn't unusual, at least not for this place. And you're not losing your mind or hallucinating or having a bad dream. I can't believe Mr. St. Jean didn't tell you about this place."

"Justin did mention something at breakfast. He said it was silly to believe in the existence of the—how did he phrase it—'the supernatural.'"

Walter laughed. "Justin St. Jean is and always will be pragmatic. But he's also wrong. You don't know the history of this place?"

"No. Please, have a seat, Walter."

Walter hesitated for a moment before taking a seat opposite her on the loveseat. "Thank you."

Marcia caught the scent of his aftershave as he sat down and the aroma lingered on her nostrils for a moment. *Aramis...I'm sure of it. He smells wonderful...*

As Walter stretched out his long lean legs, Marcia caught herself before her mind wandered. "What can you tell me about this mansion, Walter?"

"I was born and raised right here in the Quarter and the LaLaurie Mansion has always been a place of special interest to me. I've read many books about the mansion."

"Please, do tell," Marcia asked.

"I'll do my best. Let's see. The LaLaurie Mansion was built in 1832. The original property owner was a gentleman by the name of Edmond Soniet du Fossat. He had the home built for a Dr. LaLaurie. Dr. LaLaurie was not a medical doctor, but what was unusual for the time, a dentist."

"A dentist?"

"Yes. Not too many dentists in Louisiana at that time so it's believed that Dr. LaLaurie was at the top of his profession, although no one really knows for sure. Anyhow, he made quite a bit of money and climbed in social standing. Then he and his wife Delphine, a socialite in her fifties, moved into this mansion and made it one of the best showplaces in all of New Orleans. An invitation to a party here at that time was like being invited to the White House. You were in."

Walter leaned back in his chair. "As a hostess, Madame Delphine LaLaurie was a gracious and attractive woman, outgoing and charming. All reports of her indicate that she kept a beautiful home. Most of the chandeliers and woodwork you see here were added during the LaLauries' tenure. How she loved to give parties! Some said that Madame LaLaurie lived for parties. She gave the utmost care to the details, everything from the cocktails served, to the hors d'oeuvres to the dishes used to serve the dinner. Madame LaLaurie was especially picky when it came to setting her table or the proper use of china. Glasses had to match perfectly with dinner plates and so on. Flowers were fresh, as if they had been picked just moments prior to being set on the table.

"I might also mention that Madame LaLaurie's marriage to Dr. LaLaurie was her third."

"Third? She was divorced?"

"Oh, no. Not for that time, and not for a woman in society. No, her other two husbands died, both quite mysteriously, I understand. Her first husband, a Spanish gentleman named Don Ramon de Lopez y Angulo died in 1804 in Cuba. They had a daughter together, named after Madame LaLaurie whose Christian name was Marie. He died, leaving Madame LaLaurie heavily in debt. There's no record of what she did to get by during the time between her first and second husband, a slave trader named Jean Blanque. When he died eight years later, also mysteriously, he also left Madame LaLaurie in debt. I'm sure that when she married Dr. LaLaurie it was with some relief, as he was quite a wealthy man."

"So that's the woman whose portrait hangs in the hallway?"

"Yes, although most of the tenants have requested its removal. I found that portrait in the attic just a week ago and the owner decided to hang it. Thought it was fitting as this is still known as LaLaurie Mansion. Still, given the mansion's history, I should have known better. I guess the owner didn't know it would cause such a stir. I should have, though."

"Where was she from? Was she born in Louisiana?" Marcia asked.

"Yes, she was born right here into one of the most prominent New Orleans families. Her father was an Irish immigrant named McCarty and her mother was a handsome woman named Vevue something, I can't recall her last name. She was brought up in a fine home with excellent tutors and taught all the ways of polite society, things essential for a girl of her class and reputation. Then…"

Walter paused and looked at Marcia. "In the late 1790s, there is a report of her parents' murder during the slave revolt in Haiti. There's no indication as to why her parents had gone to Haiti, perhaps to start a sugar plantation, but they, along with several other slave owners, were butchered during the revolt. Some historians believe that what happened later, here in the mansion, is a direct result of the effect her parents' murder at the hands of slaves had on Madame LaLaurie."

Marcia leaned forward. "What happened in this house?"

"As I was saying before, this mansion was one of the best homes in Louisiana and an invitation to tea or to a dinner or, most importantly, to a party here was worth its weight in gold. Like most wealthy New Orleanians at the time, the LaLauries owned slaves. Most reports from visitors to the home or guests at their parties indicated that Madame LaLaurie was not the kindest woman to her slaves. She was a perfectionist; everything in the home had to be just so. Slaves were property and she viewed them as such. However, and this is odd, there were written reports of manumission."

"What's that?"

"Manumissions are documents of slaves who were given their freedom. In 1832, her name, along with her husband's, is on a document that freed one of her male house servants. There's no record of why he was freed, nor if he bought his freedom."

Walter paused to clear his throat. "But one cannot view that act of kindness as representative of Madame LaLaurie. On the whole, she demanded much from her slaves, and was quick to anger if her tea was brought in too slowly or her home not cleaned to her standards, which were quite stringent. But there was no real report of abuse until 1833 when there was gossip amongst the ladies of New Orleans society regarding her ill-treatment of her slaves."

"What kind of gossip?"

"Amongst the privileged, it was important that the lady of the house have ultimate control of her household and to be respected but still act like a lady. It was rumored that Madame LaLaurie was 'quick to temper,' which was very unladylike, especially for a woman of her social standing.

"But it wasn't until 1833 when neighbors reported observing her whipping a servant girl who then jumped to her death from the roof of the mansion that the authorities took action."

"A servant girl killed herself?"

"Yes, it seems this servant girl was called in to Madame LaLaurie's salon to comb her hair because her usual servant girl was ill. Apparently the slave girl did not comb Madame LaLaurie's hair to her satisfaction. Madame LaLaurie flew into a rage and started chasing the poor girl through the house, cow whip in hand, up and down the stairs and onto the roof, where the girl chose to jump to her death to the garden below. Neighbors were shocked and contacted the authorities."

"Who was the servant girl? Does anyone know?"

"No. Records on slaves were not as accurate as you might think. The LaLauries did not keep much of an account of the slaves they bought and sold. Troubling, considering what came later."

"Was she arrested?"

"Oh, no," Walter said, shaking his head, "At that time a white woman of her station wouldn't have been arrested. Besides, the LaLauries were close friends of the district judge. However, he was under pressure to punish them and I believe all the slaves were removed from the home and sold. Madame LaLaurie was fined three hundred dollars, a small sum by today's standards, but quite a bit for that time. Still, it was a slap on the wrist if you believe chasing that girl to her death was murder. I guess, according to the laws of the time, killing that girl wasn't actually murder. It was destruction of property."

"Slaves were considered property, right?"

"That's right. Property. Killing your slaves was destroying your property. You were the one who suffered, financially that is. But Louisiana law forbade 'ill-treatment' of slaves, thus the fine. You could whip your slaves, but not too severely, and killing them was foolish."

"But at least the rest of the slaves were safe."

"Oh no," Walter said. "Madame LaLaurie waited till the slaves were put up for auction, then coerced some relatives into buying them and then selling them back to her. It was at that time that slaves started disappearing."

"Disappearing?"

"Yes. For several years, visitors to the house reported new slaves appearing without explanation of the disappearances of the old ones. One lady, the wife of a prominent attorney, had a particular fondness for the footman, a man named Tomas, who went out of his way to make sure she came and went safely. One evening, as the story goes, some men began harassing this lady as she started toward home and the footman came to her aid and was injured. She sent Madame LaLaurie a special cake to give to him as thanks. But upon her next visit to the home, Tomas was nowhere to be seen and Madame LaLaurie said that he was getting too old to work and had been sold."

"But he hadn't been?"

"Madame LaLaurie often said she had sold her slaves, but no one knew to whom and they were never seen again. People were suspicious, but there wasn't any proof until..." Walter paused. "Until April 10, 1834."

"What happened?"

"There was a horrible fire at the LaLaurie Mansion. One of the worst at the time. Rumors were that the cook, whom Madame LaLaurie had chained to the kitchen stove, had set the fire."

"She chained her cook to the stove?"

"Yes. The cook had attempted to escape several times and so the solution was to simply chain her to the stove. Unable to escape, she set the kitchen on fire. That night, the fire was raging inside the mansion when neighbors and firemen arrived. Madame LaLaurie, with her husband, was busy bringing out valuables. She entreated the neighbors to help save her furniture and paintings. But the neighbors were concerned for the well-being of those who still might be trapped inside. They asked of the slaves' whereabouts and when Madame LaLaurie indicated that they had all left already and were safe, neighbors and firemen were suspicious. They stormed the house and found a door burned down that led to the third floor attic. When they walked into that room, they found a horrible sight.

"According to the newspaper at the time, the *New Orleans Bee,* they found the slaves in the attic, all naked and all dead except for one. All had been tortured and mutilated. One poor woman was housed in a dog cage and barely alive. Her arms and legs had been broken and then set in 'various angles, this way and that.' Another slave's body had a portion of his skull removed and according to the paper, there was a stick beside him that had been used 'to stir his brain.' Other slave bodies, naked and gutted, were hanging from the walls. Other bodies were on the floor, bound in chains. All had been tortured and mutilated."

"Oh my God," Marcia gasped, clutching her stomach.

"I apologize. I should have warned you the details were quite grisly. Are you all right?"

Marcia nodded. "Yes, please go on."

"The firemen and neighbors were so revolted, they hurried from the room. Some were physically ill. All vowed that what they'd seen in the attic was the most horrible thing they had ever witnessed. When other neighbors heard of what the firemen had discovered, a lynch mob quickly formed and a rope was readied for Madame and Dr. LaLauries' necks. But they had already escaped and were never seen again."

"They escaped? How?"

"They somehow got word of the lynch mob, climbed into their carriage and got a boat across Lake Pontchartrain. After that, some say they went to France. Some say they fled to another part of Louisiana. No one really knows for sure."

"What do you think?"

"I think she stayed in Louisiana and hid out with friends or relatives. Madame LaLaurie was born and raised here. I doubt she would have left."

"What of the living slaves?"

"They were sold at auction."

"Who were they?"

Walter shook his head. "I don't know. There's an auction notice some-where, Perhaps in an old newspaper that indicated their sale, but as to who they were, we'll never know."

"And this house?"

"After the fire, it lay in disrepair for a number of years. Given what happened, no one wanted to live here. Rumors of hauntings began soon after the fire."

"What kind of hauntings?"

"Sounds of moaning, and then later, when the mansion became a boarding house, several tenants complained of encountering strange enti-ties in the hallway. One man awoke in the middle of the night to find the hands of an apparent slave wrapped tightly about his throat. According to him, another slave pushed the hands away."

"Do you think the house is haunted?"

"I know it is."

Marcia shook her head. "So what I heard was real."

"Sightings of Madame LaLaurie have been reported as well."

"Really? But she didn't die here."

"Marcia, a person doesn't have to die in a place to haunt it. Many believe that a person haunts a place that is significant to them. This house was such a place for Madame LaLaurie."

"Was she insane?"

"She must have been in order to do that to her slaves."

"Maybe it was Dr. LaLaurie."

"Some rumors say that it was both of them. After all, how could a man live in a house with all of that going on and not know about it? I guess we'll never know for sure."

"Can I ask you a personal question?"

"Of course."

"Have you ever seen a ghost?"

"No."

"So why do you believe this place is haunted?"

"I've never seen anything, but I've heard things in the night, and I'm a deep sleeper. One night, I was woken up by loud tapping noises."

"Tapping?"

"Yeah, like someone was tapping their foot. I thought it might be one of the tenants, so I got up and when I opened the door and stepped out into the hallway, I didn't see or hear anybody. I listened, but the tapping noise had stopped. So I went back to bed. As soon as I was back in bed, I heard the tapping noise again, but this time it was even louder and more persistent, as if someone had purposely waited for me to return to bed before tapping again. I got up again and went out into the hallway. Still nothing. Then, just as I was turning to go back into bed, I heard the tapping again, distinctive, on the staircase. I walked over and called out, but no one answered. But I could still hear the tapping noise, like someone was coming up the steps."

"What was it?"

"I don't know. I never heard anything after that night. That's kind of what got me so curious about the mansion. I read through some of the history of the mansion and discovered a case of a haunting in the late 1800s. A man reported being confronted on the staircase by the ghost of a badly mutilated slave, his hands bound in chains that tapped against the staircase as he climbed up toward the attic."

"Is that what you think you heard?"

"It's possible."

"But what can be done?"

"Nothing."

"There must be something that can be done."

"I wouldn't worry too much about the ghosts of LaLaurie Mansion. They ask for things that don't exist. You can't help them. Whoever this woman is, she's probably been asking for help for a long time, long before you or I came."

"So shouldn't someone help her?"

"How can you help her?"

"Find out who she is, who Sam is, perhaps."

"You're going to help a ghost?"

"I know it sounds silly, but I feel something for this woman, a connection. I can't explain it. I don't know her, but I want to help her. If I can."

Walter shrugged his shoulders, but his eyes grew soft as he looked at her. "I admire you for wanting to help, but she's just a ghost. I don't know how you can be of any help to a ghost."

"Maybe I can find Sam."

"But you don't even know who Sam is."

"I can find out. If you'll help me."

"Oh, no, not me." Walter shook his head and stood. "I'll leave the ghost hunting to you, ma'am. I'd better get back—"

"Please," Marcia said as she grabbed his arm. She felt him quiver as her fingers touched his muscled arm and he turned to look at her. The moment their eyes met, Marcia felt warmth course through her body. Walter's eyes moved slowly from her eyes to take in the length of her body. Marcia was aware of his eyes on her and felt the warmth reach her most intimate place. Walter Dufrane was making it hard for her to concentrate.

"Please," Marcia said again, letting go of his arm and standing up. "You know so much about New Orleans. I wouldn't know where to begin."

"I don't go out much, like to keep to home."

"Please, Walter, I need your help."

Walter considered her entreaty for a moment. "All right. If you want to go on a ghost hunt, then I'll help you if I can."

"Thank you," Marcia said with some relief.

"Where do you want to start?"

"First, we need to find out more about this ghost who is asking for Sam."

Walter shook his head as he walked to the door. "That will be difficult. They're not too many records left from that time. Most of the LaLauries' personal papers were destroyed in the fire."

"Where do you think we should begin?"

Walter thought for a moment. "Let's go down to the main library and look at the microfiche. They have old copies of the *New Orleans Bee* from that time. Maybe we can learn more about the fire."

"Really?"

"Yes."

Marcia smiled at him. "You're really going to help me, aren't you?"

"Yes, I will. I promise I'll help."

"Great."

"Now," Walter said as he opened the door, "don't get your hopes up. We'll probably come up with nothing."

"At least we can try. Thanks, Walter."

"Wait a minute now."

"What is it?" she asked.

"What if this ghost visits you again tonight?"

"I'll listen...very carefully. See if I can find something out."

"All right." Walter extended his hand and as they touched, Marcia felt electricity course through her body. She pulled her hand away, sure that he knew that she was attracted to him. When she looked up into his hazel eyes, she felt her heart race for a moment. He smiled hesitantly. "Be careful. Probably only the living can harm you, but you never know."

"I'll be fine. I know the woman speaking to me doesn't want to hurt me. Where shall I meet you?" she asked.

"Here of course," he said as he stepped out into the hallway. He paused in the doorway. "Marcia—"

"Yes?"

"Sorry about earlier. When I'm at the piano...I apologize for being rude."

Marcia smiled. "Apology accepted."

He stuck out his hand. "Friends?"

She felt her heart drop at that word. The last thing in the world she wanted was to be merely friends with the handsome and captivating man, but she smiled and extended her own hand. "Friends."

Walter shook her hand, and Marcia noticed that his hand was warm and engulfed hers completely, and when they let go, his hand shook a little. He nodded good-bye and she watched as he went inside his apartment and shut the door.

⁓

A few moments later, Walter was back inside his own apartment. He shut the door and walked over to the couch and sat down, and as he did, his eyes fell on the picture of his wife, Florence, that rested on the coffee table. He picked it up and held it for a moment before wiping some dust from the frame with the end of his shirt and replacing it onto the table. He turned back toward the door and thought of the woman he had conversed with moments before. The thought of her sitting there in her robe, soft and vulnerable, made his heart race. Not since Florence had he met a woman who made him feel the way Marcia Watkins did. Her passion to help the ghost find Sam had him intrigued and excited about something for the first time in a long time. He smiled as he recalled her warm smile and beautiful long legs.

He glanced down at his hands and saw that they were still shaking. *Calm down, you fool.* Taking a sip of water from a glass on the table, he kicked off his shoes and stretched out on the sofa. As he gazed at the picture of his wife, he felt guilty. *Why am I thinking about Marcia? What about Flo?* Thoughts of Marcia began to drift away as images of Flo, her soft hands and sweet kisses, flooded his mind. *I miss you, baby.* It had been two years since Florence died and thinking about her brought an aching pain in Walter's chest. He twisted the wedding band on his finger and closed his eyes. *Don't worry, baby...I'll never love anyone like I loved you...there'll never be anyone for me except you.*

CHAPTER SIX

As Marcia stood in the shower washing off the soap, she thought of Walter Dufrane. A smile came to her lips as she recalled his smooth, mocha skin and his soft-looking lips. *He is so handsome.* She sighed, though, as she recalled his straightforward, neighborly shake of her hand. *He's not interested in me. Still...* She hadn't noticed a wedding band on his finger, but that didn't mean he wasn't married. Many men she worked with refused to wear wedding bands, but Walter did not strike her as that kind of man. *How would you know?* a voice asked. *You don't even know what kind of man he is.*

She turned off the water and got out. As she dried herself off and rubbed lotion on her body, she couldn't shake the image of Walter from her mind. She had always loved intelligent men and Walter was certainly that. He seemed to be well-read, especially about New Orleans history. She found intelligence like that sexy, much sexier than money or a fancy car, which had never turned her on as it did other women. As she towel-dried her hair, she again smiled to herself. She did want a man in her life, but not so he could support her, rather for companionship, a man to love and hold her, and make her feel special.

As she dressed, she decided to get to know Walter Dufrane, even if it was just as friends. There was just something about him that made her quiver with childlike excitement.

A few minutes later, she went for a walk around the French Quarter. As she walked, she couldn't help wondering what the French Quarter might have been like when the slave woman was living there. As she glanced up at the old buildings, she thought that the Quarter had probably not changed that much at all. Marcia sighed as she walked past the antique shops and stopped in Café Beignet for a café au lait and a chocolate éclair. As she ate, she thought about the ghost woman's desperate plea. At the same time, she felt guilty that she wasn't paying more attention to her sister's wedding. She was worried about Anna, but somehow, those thoughts had been pushed to the back of her mind. Now, in less than two days, she was wrapped up in a mystery, one she could not forget and one which she was determined to solve before she left New Orleans.

As she sipped her coffee, she was glad that Walter had agreed to help her. She wouldn't have known where to begin research in a strange city. She didn't want to get hopeful, but he'd seemed excited by the whole mystery of the slave woman. Was it only curiosity? Or did he want to get to know her better? In the back of her mind and her heart, she hoped that Walter Dufrane was interested in more than just a mystery.

She paid for her coffee and éclair and found herself wandering onto Jackson Square, named after President Andrew Jackson. As she watched the street performers, she spotted a nearby bookstore and decided to go in. There were hundreds of old books on the shelves and as she wandered down the aisles, she found one that outlined the history of the French Quarter from the late 1700s to present day. What caught her eye was the picture of LaLaurie Mansion on the cover. The index listed several pages that discussed LaLaurie Mansion. After buying the book, she walked down Pirate's Alley toward Royal Street. Just outside the William Faulkner House, she stopped. As she stared up at the little apartment where Faulkner wrote *Soldier's Pay*, she was suddenly aware of eyes on her. She turned, but found herself alone in the alley, except for a group of Japanese tourists who were photographing a painter. Nevertheless, she couldn't shake the feeling that she was being watched and quickly left Pirate's Alley. A heavy feeling hung over her all the way back to the mansion.

From the outside, the mansion looked peaceful, innocent, but Marcia knew it held secrets that revealed themselves only at night. She glanced at the clock as she entered her room and realized that she had only an hour to get ready for dinner. Examining the dresser drawers, she saw that they were as she'd left them. Apparently the slave woman had decided not to pay her another surprise visit. Only when she breathed a sigh of relief and relaxed did she realize that her fists had been tightly clenched. She knew she needed to unwind so after turning on the hot water, she opened the French doors and sat on the balcony as she waited for the tub to fill. Down below, in an impromptu jazz session, three men were playing Duke Ellington's "Take the A Train." She tapped her fingers in time to the music, glorying in the quaintness and charm of the Crescent City. But when she went back inside to check on the water level, she saw that the dresser drawers were all open and felt the icy cold of the room. She stood rooted, frantically scanning the room, but she saw and heard nothing. Then, fearful the water would overflow the tub, she hurried into the bathroom and shut the door, locking it. Deriding herself for her fears, she took a long bath and emerged a half hour later in her robe. The dresser drawers were once again closed.

Walter sat at the dining table, eating his steak and potatoes. Across from him, as it had been for the past two years, was a place setting for Florence. It didn't make sense, he knew, to set out a place setting for her, but it made him feel less lonely. He ate slowly, glancing across at the setting every once in a while. The food tasted bland and he washed it down with a gulp of wine. He poured himself another glass and took turns taking a bit of meat and then washing it down with the wine. He wished that Flo were there, sitting across from him, taking dainty bites of her dinner as she talked on about her day. He smiled to himself, remembering how his plate would be scraped clean before she had even taken her first bite. They had been opposites in that way, but had complemented each other in other ways.

He poured himself another glass of wine and then stood up to clear the table. Cleaning up after dinner was much faster these days. No more complicated meals with hard-to-pronounce recipes. Just a simple meat or a piece of fish with vegetables. He really didn't see a need to cook anything fancy when it was just him.

Florence had loved gourmet food, and more than that, gourmet recipes. He glanced over at the kitchen bookshelf and saw the cookbooks lining the shelves. As he rinsed his plate, and then the frying pan, he thought of all their visits to bookstores, searching for new and exotic cookbooks such as *How to Cook Indian Cuisine, The Minimalist* and *Ethnic Gourmet.* They still had a place on the shelf. Placing the plate and pan into the dishwasher, he thought of making dinner with Flo. He smiled as he recalled her difficulty in pronouncing some of the ingredients in the new recipes she was always experimenting with.

They each had a specific duty when it came to making dinner. She would clean and cut vegetables while he opened a bottle of wine and poured them each a glass. Then he would put in a Miles Davis CD while she made a salad. Flo loved fish for dinner, whatever was fresh at the market that day. He loved watching her prepare dinner, a cookbook propped open while she perused the recipe. He'd refill her wine glass and laugh as she struggled to get just the right amount of tarragon on the trout or sumac on the ground meat. Sometimes Flo would get really creative and cook an entire ethnic meal, like the time she made Peking duck with steamed pork dumplings.

Taking another sip of his wine, he fondly remembered how he would set the table and help bring food to the table when it was ready. Florence's smile was the thing he missed most. She could make him smile even when he was mad at her for something. How he missed her fragrant perfume wafting in the air, her soft hands and her laughter.

There was a knock and Marcia, dressed in black slacks, blouse, and sandals, met Justin and Anna at the door.

"Good evening," Justin said as he and Anna entered. "You're look-ing quite lovely tonight, Marcia."

"Thank you."

"Your room is to your satisfaction?" he asked as he glanced around the room.

"Yes. Very comfortable."

"Wonderful. No more ghosts?"

Marcia looked from Justin to Anna and then back at him before answering. She knew that sharing what she had experienced that after-noon would only cause Justin to ridicule her, so she put a fake smile on her face as she wrapped her shawl about her shoulders. "Nope, not that I saw anyway." It wasn't exactly a lie. She had never actually *seen* the woman whose voice filled her room. But she was determined to help her, any way she could.

All through dinner, as Anna prattled on about finding the perfect dress, Marcia smiled and pretended to listen. Her thoughts, however, were on Walter Dufrane. The memory of his penetrating eyes made her pulse race. She took a sip of her wine and played with the baked cat-fish on her plate, all the while wishing that it were morning and she could be meeting him again.

"You seem far away tonight, Marcia."

Marcia glanced over at Justin and smiled. "Am I? I hadn't noticed."

Justin took a drink of wine and nodded. "Yes. Is there something on your mind?"

Marcia shook her head. "Just thoughts of the wedding." She reached out and took Anna's hand in hers. "I'm very happy for my sister and I want her wedding day to be special."

Justin smiled and reached over, removing Anna's hand from Marcia's and cupping it in his own hand possessively. "It will be. You needn't worry."

Anna blushed happily as Justin placed his arm around her shoul-ders and pulled her toward him. He looked at Marcia as Anna let her head rest on his shoulder. Marcia suddenly knew what it all meant and she didn't like it. Justin was marking his territory, making sure that

Marcia knew that Anna was his, one hundred percent. She glanced at Anna, but Anna seemed to be unaware of what was going on. Justin smiled at her over the top of Anna's head, his arms clasped tightly around Anna.

"If you don't mind me saying so, it's a shame you're not married. You're an attractive woman…for your age."

For my age! She wanted to smack Justin St. Jean in his smug face, but she restrained herself.

"Justin, that's rude!" Anna admonished.

"I apologize, that certainly wasn't my intention."

"That's all right, Justin. I just haven't found Mr. Right yet. Not as lucky as my sister, I suppose," she said this through gritted teeth, all the while looking directly at Justin.

Justin met her look and held Anna tighter. "Perhaps."

Anna pulled slightly away. "How can you be so mean to my sister, Justin?"

Justin laughed and grabbed Anna's cheeks like a mother would a baby. "Have I upset you, darling? No matter, I know how to remedy that." Justin pulled a black oval jewelry box from his pocket and slowly slid it over the table toward her. Anna gasped with glee as she hurriedly pulled the ribbon away from the top and opened the box to reveal a spectacular diamond bracelet.

"Oh, Justin," Anna said as she grasped the bracelet in her hand. "It's so beautiful."

"Just like you, my precious darling. Here, allow me." Justin kissed Anna and helped her put on the bracelet. As Marcia watched Anna gaze down at the bracelet, Justin met her eyes and the look in his spoke volumes. Justin St. Jean was now in control, and there wasn't anything Marcia could do about it.

Marcia watched as they embraced, and she smiled at Anna across the table, more determined than ever to have another nice long talk with her sister before she made that walk down the aisle.

They walked from the restaurant over to the Louis Armstrong, which was packed with customers. It was a small place, kind of a dive, but Marcia liked the vibe and the terrific music. A jazz band was in full swing as they were seated at a table near the front. Glancing over at Justin, Marcia could see that he was uncomfortable. The place was a bit noisy, full of drinking college boys, tourists, and locals. Although the cigarette smoke set her to coughing, it wasn't going to deter her from having fun.

"Do you like it?"

"It's great! But how could you work in all this noise and madness?"

"I loved it."

Marcia didn't miss that word. "Loved?"

But Anna was preoccupied with waving at the waitress. She hurried over and hugged Anna. Marcia was introduced to the waitress, Sheryl. Sheryl admired Anna's new bracelet and then took their order. Marcia and Anna both ordered scotch and sodas while Justin asked for a Galliano.

Sheryl laughed and shook her head. "We don't have that. I think you tried to order that last time you were here, too."

Justin gave the woman a look that said he did not appreciate her comment, then cleared his throat. "I'll have what the ladies are having then."

"You going to come and see us from time to time, Anna?"

"I will. Don't worry, Sheryl."

Sheryl smiled and went off to get the drinks. Marcia leaned into Anna. It was hard to talk above the music in the room. "What was that all about?"

"Oh nothing. Don't worry about it. Isn't the music great?"

"Terrific."

Marcia again looked over at Justin, who was surveying the scene with a look of distaste. While she had to admit she wasn't exactly into New York-style dive bars, it was where her sister worked and she was going to put on a happy face for Anna. Why couldn't Justin?

Sheryl returned with their drinks and Justin pulled out money to pay her. Sheryl shook her head and pointed to the bar where a hulking man was pouring drinks. "It's on the house. On Ed."

Anna smiled and waved over at Ed. "Tell him thanks!"

"I will."

As Sheryl left, Marcia saw Justin give Anna a look. She didn't know what it meant, but Anna's smile slid from her face and she dropped her head and sipped her drink. As they listened to the music, one by one Anna's coworkers came over to greet her and to meet Marcia. They simply nodded at Justin, with whom they were obviously acquainted, but did not offer greetings.

"I'm happy to see you have so many wonderful friends and coworkers. This must be a great place to work. And to think I was worried about you waitressing."

"Yeah," Anna said wistfully.

The band finished their number to thunderous applause. The hulking man came out from behind the bar and took the stage. Anna leaned over to Marcia. "That's Ed, the owner."

"Oh?"

"Yeah, he handles the bar on crazy nights like this."

"Hmm…maybe you could talk to him tonight."

Anna gave her a look. "About what?"

"You know, what we talked about before. You singing. It seems like a perfect night for it. We're here for moral support."

"No. Just drop it, Marcia. I'm not asking him."

"But—"

Justin looked from Anna to Marcia. "What's all this about? What are you going to ask, Anna?"

Anna gave Marcia a look. "Nothing, Justin. It's nothing."

Ed took the stage and bowed as applause again filled the room. He quieted down the crowd and then addressed them. "Folks, I hope you're enjoying The New Time Twisters. Let's hear it for them!"

Again the crowd erupted into applause.

"Thank you. Now, I know it isn't Amateur Night, but we have a special lady amongst us who's been begging me for a chance to come up here and sing for you. She's getting married next week, so as an early wedding gift, Anna Watkins, would you come on up here?"

Anna gasped and looked first at Justin and then Marcia. Marcia applauded the loudest of anyone in the audience.

"Anna! Come on, Anna! Audience! Let's give her some encouragement! Put your hands together for her!"

The audience clapped loudly, waiting for Anna to ascend the stage. Marcia shoved her a bit, encouraging her to get up. "Come on, Anna, this is your chance. Go on."

Anna looked over at Justin. He shook his head. "Perhaps this is not the proper time."

Anna then glanced over at Marcia who encouraged her with another friendly shove in the direction of the stage. "Ignore him. Go on." She and Justin exchanged a look. Why was he being so difficult?

Anna then hopped up and walked to the stage. Ed helped her up and handed a microphone to her. The New Time Twisters came back on stage and readied their instruments. "Anna, what'll it be?"

"I…I'll sing Billie Holiday's 'Solitude'."

"The stage is yours." Ed hugged Anna, then got down. The music started up and Anna began singing. Her voice was breathtaking, sweet and subtle as she sang Billie's song and the crowd was hushed as they listened. Afterwards, they erupted in applause and with their encouragement, she sang another, this time "Fine and Mellow," which told of a woman's complaints about the mistreatment she was receiving at the hands of her "man." The audience was really into that one, snapping their fingers and tapping their feet, but when Marcia glanced over at Justin, she could see he was angry. Either the song lyrics or Anna had him steaming. Marcia leaned over to him.

"She doesn't mean you, it's just a song," she began.

"I am well aware that it's just a song, thank you," Justin snapped.

Marcia sat back, a little shocked by his abruptness. *Why is he acting this way? Isn't he at all happy for Anna? This is what she's always wanted.* As the song ended, Marcia clapped as loudly as she could, to make sure Anna knew that at least she was happy for her. Anna bowed and got down off the stage. When she returned to the table, Marcia hugged her. "I'm so proud of you. That was wonderful. You've got real talent."

Anna beamed and looked at Justin, who abruptly stood up. "Are we ready to leave now?"

Obviously surprised, Anna smiled to cover her disappointment. Justin left a tip on the table and they headed to the door. Along the way, members of the audience kept grabbing Anna's hand to congratulate her. As Justin held the door open, Marcia heard him mutter underneath his breath, "I'm thankful I'll never have to grace the door of such an establishment again."

＊

Justin and Anna had nothing to say on the walk back to Royal Street. He clearly was not happy that Anna had gone on stage, making Marcia wonder if Anna had ever discussed her desire to be a singer with him. *Probably not.* Apparently Justin St. Jean was displeased by anything that didn't directly involve him or his decisions.

At the corner of Royal Street, she stopped.

"I'll walk from here. I need some fresh air."

She hugged Anna and congratulated her again. They made plans to meet at a coffee shop in the Central Business District to look for wedding and bridesmaid dresses. They were running out of time to choose their dresses and get them altered.

"Be careful. The French Quarter is relatively safe, but watch yourself," Justin cautioned.

"I will," she said as she looked at Justin, holding his eyes with her own for a second. She wanted to say something to him about Anna.

"You know, Justin," she began, "it might be nice if you and I could meet for coffee sometime this week, without Anna, so we could get to know one another. I mean, I really don't know anything about you, and well, Anna is my only sister."

Justin held up his hand. "I've already made such arrangements. Tomorrow evening, there is to be a cocktail party followed by dinner at my family's estate. There, you will be properly introduced to the members of my family."

"Oh?" Marcia was surprised.

"I'd have thought Anna would have told you."

"I think she did, didn't you, Anna?"

Anna nodded, but seemed a million miles away.

"Yes, it'll be a grand affair," Justin said as he leaned over to kiss her good night on the cheek. He was all charm and sophistication once again, but this time, Marcia wasn't buying into the act. Justin St. Jean was a complicated fellow. One minute, a perfect gentleman, the other minute, an angry, possessive fellow who pouted like a child if he didn't get his own way.

"At the party we'll have a chance to sit and get to know one another. It's my desire to know you, Marcia."

"Me too," Marcia replied.

Justin smiled as he took Anna's hand. "Take care."

Marcia waved good-bye as they walked off to the garage where Justin kept his car. Her heart was heavy as she walked down Royal Street to the mansion. Justin did not seem to know or care about Anna's dream of singing. She had known Justin for only couple of days, yet she already mistrusted him. She didn't know what Anna wanted with such an obviously controlling man, but as she walked toward LaLaurie Mansion, she doubted Anna would ever have a chance at a singing career once she became his wife.

As she approached the dark corner where the mansion sat, she felt a chill run up her spine. She stopped and looked up at the third floor window. Unlike the other windows in the house, the windows were shuttered on that side. She suddenly blinked and rubbed her eyes. *I'm not seeing what I'm seeing.*

But there, on the third floor balcony, Marcia could see a distinctive green glow move from one end of the balcony to the other end. She blinked again and squinting, peered up at the form. It paused, hanging in mid air before moving to the other end of the balcony, where it again paused. Marcia stood transfixed, tightly clutching her evening bag as she stared up at the balcony.

"Are you all right there?" a voice from behind her asked.

Marcia practically jumped when she heard the voice. "What?"

"Sorry, didn't mean to startle you."

Marcia turned around to see an older woman dressed in a maid's uniform smiling at her.

"Just wanted to see if you were all right."

"Oh yes," Marcia replied, her voice cracking. "I was just...just having a look at the mansion."

The woman looked up at the mansion and just shook her head. "I work over there at the Bourbon Orleans hotel. Been working over there for going on thirty years. Every day, I park right across the street from this old place, 'cause it's the only place I can find parking. Every night when I get off work, I got to walk past this place to get to my car. Every night, I dread it. You want to know why?"

"Why?" Marcia asked.

"Because that place is haunted...and not in any good way neither."

"Is there a good way for a place to be haunted?"

"Sure there is," the woman said. "Sometimes a place be haunted because someone love someone and ain't willing to go to the other side without them. Sometimes, 'cause they still lonely and other times 'cause they don't know they're dead. But not the way that old place is haunted. There was some awful stuff done up in there to our people, folks just like us, and there ain't no forgivin' nor forgettin'."

"Have you ever seen anything?"

"Nope, and I don't aim to either. I hear stories, though, of people who've stayed there and well, they've seen some things."

"You've never been inside?"

"Oh no," the woman said, shaking her head emphatically. "Not me. Couldn't get in anyway. That place is closed to the public."

"I'm staying there."

"You are? Why?"

"My brother-in-law owns an apartment in there."

"Have you seen anything?"

Marcia paused and looked at the woman before answering. "Maybe."

The woman shook her head. "There's no way I'd stay in there. You couldn't pay me. You see that hotel over there?" The woman pointed to a building on the next corner.

"Yes?"

"That's where I work. That used to be the Quadroon Ballroom."

"Quadroon Ballroom?"

"Yes, where rich white men and Creole gentleman could go and choose a mistress, with her momma's blessing. Mistresses were all free women of color, quadroons."

"Really? And now it's a hotel. I didn't know that."

"That's right. After the ballroom shut down, the place became a girls' school and then changed hands a few different times before being a hotel. To tell the truth, it's kind of creepy sometimes, workin' in that building at night, cleaning the rooms and all, seeing as it's such an old building, but I'll take it over that mansion any day of the week. You take care now and watch the traffic when you cross the street. Drivers in this city be crazy. They don't stop for no pedestrians."

With that, the woman waved and crossed the street to her car. Marcia looked up at the mansion again, but seeing nothing, she got out her key and went inside.

The first thing she noticed was that the Madame LaLaurie portrait had been removed and replaced with a portrait of St. Louis Cathedral. As she walked slowly up the stairs, her breath caught at the back of her throat. She derided herself for being afraid. *The dead can't hurt you, not like the living.*

She walked inside the apartment and glanced nervously around the room. She was determined to help the ghost, no matter what, but the idea that the ghost would once again approach her both scared and intrigued her. She wanted to know more about this ghost and her search for "Sam."

Getting into bed, she pulled the covers over her body, left the bedside lamp on and waited for something to happen. After a few uneventful minutes passed, she fell asleep.

It was the cold air that awoke her. She immediately knew that she wasn't alone in the room. Slowly, she lifted her head and for the first time saw the person associated with the mysterious voice. There, standing by the bed, was a light-skinned woman, very beautiful, with her head wrapped in a turban of some kind. She was dressed in a long, plain gown that flowed all the way to her bare feet. But the woman's hands were tied behind her back and she suffered from a horrible wound which had laid open her stomach. Marcia gasped and held her hand to her mouth as she saw that the woman's insides were spilling out. The woman moaned and stared at Marcia.

"What do you want?" Marcia asked.

The woman said nothing but moaned again.

"Sam? Do you want me to find Sam?"

The woman stopped moaning and nodded her head. Marcia shivered as the woman stared at her for another moment. Then, just like that, she was gone.

Marcia lay back on the pillow as the temperature in the room rose to normal. She was shaking, but she had come face-to-face with the ghost. She swallowed down bile as she recalled the horrible wound to the woman's stomach. *That's how she must have died.* The woman must have been one of Madame LaLaurie's unfortunate servants. Perhaps Sam was another slave like her, a slave who had met his death in the mansion. As she shut her eyes, she made a mental note to see if she and Walter could find any records regarding the slaves at LaLaurie Mansion. If she found a "Sam," perhaps she could uncover the identity of the slave woman. Whoever she was, she seemed determined not to go to her resting place without Sam.

CHAPTER SEVEN

Marcia sat bolt upright in bed when she heard the knock on her door. She'd had horrible nightmares all night and was exhausted.

"Yes?"

"It's Walter, Marcia. Are you ready to go to the library?"

"No," Marcia called. She jumped up, threw on her robe and hurried to open the door, pulling the robe tighter as she went. The sight of Walter dressed in a pair of khaki pants and a cream-colored shirt set her head spinning. Embarrassment heated her face, though, when she thought about her uncombed hair and general state of disarray.

"I didn't wake you, did I?" Leaning up against the doorjamb and crossing his arms, Walter stuck out his hand and they shook. Marcia again felt that spark of electricity run through her body. The man was so enticing. How could someone look so good just wearing a pair of pants and simple shirt? His intoxicating aftershave floated to her and she swallowed a couple of times to try to gain control of her emotions.

"Uh, yes, I apologize. But…"

"Rough night?"

Marcia nodded. "Yes. Quite a night. Come on in. I'll just be a few minutes."

Walter came in and sat down while Marcia dashed into the bathroom and threw on a pair of jeans and shirt. She washed her face and quickly tied her hair back into a tight updo, then applied some foundation, powder, eyeliner, and lipstick. She could have kicked herself for sleeping late and not leaving enough time to get ready. Sighing, she opened the bathroom door and faced Walter.

"Thanks for coming with me today," she said. Just then she noticed that Walter wore a wedding band. Her heart sank. *No wonder he wants to be friends…he's married.* She caught Walter staring at her so she smiled to mask her disappointment and pulled on her sandals. "You mind if we stop for coffee on the way? I barely had any sleep last night."

Walter stood as Marcia got her purse. "I'll treat you to coffee and beignets before we set off to the library. I only have a couple of hours this morning before I meet with the board, but I'm all yours until then. Does that suit you?"

As Marcia processed the words *I'm all yours,* she felt her heart skip a beat. But she simply nodded her head and tried to focus her thoughts on the business at hand.

Café Du Monde was packed as usual, but they were finally able to secure a seat in a quiet corner inside. They ordered beignets and coffee. As they waited, Marcia pulled a small notepad and pen out of her purse.

"Look at you, the master detective at work already," Walter said, smiling. He liked an organized woman.

"It's not really what it looks like. I'm an interior designer by trade and I always carry around a notepad and pen in case during a walk-through with a client they have some ideas they want me to jot down."

"How long have you been an interior designer?"

"Since I graduated from Parsons School of Design."

"So you would be around…?"

Marcia looked at him curiously. "What are you digging for?"

Walter shifted in his seat. "That was rude of me, forgive me."

Marcia laughed. "You want to know my age?"

"As a matter of fact I do. I'm sorry if my question is rude, but you look awfully young."

Marcia felt her face grow warm, but on the inside she was beaming. She'd never received such a compliment before. She saw Walter's eyes on her face, waiting for an answer.

"Fifteen years. I've been a designer for fifteen years."

"So that would make you…thirty-five?"

"Thirty-seven. And you?"

"I'm forty-three, but you can tell me I look young for my age."

Marcia laughed. When he wanted, Walter Dufrane could be quite charming. "You do. You look great," Marcia said hesitantly, suddenly too aware of Walter. He seemed to squirm uncomfortably under her gaze, but the question on the tip of her tongue slipped out before she could control it.

"So you're married?"

Walter ignored the question as the waitress, a petite Chinese woman, appeared with a tray loaded with two plates of fresh beignets, two big cups of coffee and two glasses of water. Walter paid her and they dug in. Tasting a beignet, Marcia was again amazed at the delicate sweetness of the dough, which was complemented by sugar on top. She took a sip of her coffee, careful not to burn her tongue, and stole a glance at Walter across the table. *Why didn't he answer me? It's obvious he's married if he's wearing a wedding band.* After a moment, Walter cleared his throat and met her gaze with a penetrating look. Marcia felt that familiar warmth in her intimate place and she fought to control the urge to lean across the table and kiss him. *I wonder what it would be like to kiss him? Wonderful...*

"Are you?"

"Am I what?" His question jolted her out of her fantasy.

"Married."

She shook her head. "No."

"Divorced?"

"Nope. Never been married."

"I find that hard to believe."

"Why?"

"That nobody has swept a beautiful woman like you away."

So he is interested! Resisting the urge to jump up on the table and dance for joy, she smiled and took a sip of coffee. "They might have wanted to, but I guess I never gave them a chance." It wasn't exactly the truth, but she didn't want to tell Walter that men didn't stick around long enough to get to know her, let alone ask her to marry them.

"I was too busy starting my own business. It takes up a lot of my time," she added.

"You have your own interior design company?"

"Yes," Marcia replied proudly. "Marcia Watkins Interior Design, Ltd. I'm real proud of that. It's kind of what paid the bills for a while after my parents died."

"Oh, I'm sorry."

Marcia nodded, feeling silly that tears were welling up at the mention of her parents. She looked over at Walter's hand. "It's all right. How long have you been married?"

"Me?"

Marcia saw a sad look come across Walter's face and he grew contemplative. He delicately touched the wedding band. "I'm not..."

Marcia felt her heart soar. *He's not married!*

"...married, technically. I'm widowed. My wife, Florence, died of cancer two years ago. We were high school sweethearts."

"I'm sorry."

"Thank you. I guess that's why I'm such a homebody. 'There just ain't no living without you.' That was an expression we'd use and it's true in a way. She was my everything."

Walter looked closely at Marcia. "I've never met anyone I thought could replace her. She was a very special woman."

"I bet she was."

"You know what I regret most?"

"What's that?"

"Not having children with her. She wanted them right away, but I kept telling her the timing wasn't right. 'Next year.' Now all I have to remind me of her are a few pictures."

"Was she very beautiful?"

"Yes, and a gifted pianist. I play piano, went to the conservatory, but I don't play like her..."

He paused, and Marcia could see that he was struggling to find the words to express his love for Florence. "We lived for one another. Each day with her was so special, an adventure. She loved to laugh and talk. But when she got sick, I was so busy, so damn busy." He looked at her and Marcia saw tears in his eyes. "I'm sorry, I don't know why I'm telling you all this."

"No, please, go on," Marcia urged.

"It was my dream to open a piano/jazz bar. I wanted a place where Flo could showcase her talents as a pianist, a place we could run together. I imagined a place like Preservation Hall, but with a nice long bar and lounge chairs. It was my dream, but I kept telling her that I was doing it for both us. I got so caught up with opening Flo's Joint, that I didn't realize how sick she was. She hadn't been feeling well for a while, but I just thought she was stressed out. Sometimes she'd sleep all day and still feel tired. I was so preoccupied with the business, that I think she stopped coming to me. That place put a lot of strain on our marriage, financially and emotionally. Flo kept telling me we should think about postponing the opening of Flo's Joint, but I didn't listen. Then we found out she had cancer. All of a sudden, everything slipped away, all our problems, everything, and all I could think about was Flo getting better. She had to live, I told myself. She had to. What was I going to do without her?"

Walter looked over at Marcia and the look in his eyes spoke volumes. "But it was too late. The cancer had already spread. She died six months later."

"Oh, Walter." Before Marcia realized what she was doing, she reached out and took his hand. "I'm so sorry."

Walter nodded. "I still feel so guilty. Why did I let the damn business come in the way of us? Why?"

"You shouldn't blame yourself."

"Then who should I blame?"

Marcia shrugged. "Sometimes these things are beyond our control."

Walter shook his head. "I don't know about that. If I hadn't been so selfish, Flo would be here now."

"You don't know that, Walter."

Walter shook his head and looked away.

"What happened to Flo's Joint?" Marcia asked.

"I never opened it. Even after all that work, it just didn't seem to matter. The place was for her, for us, and it wasn't the same without her."

Walter took a sip of water and cleared his throat. "Do you want to know what I really miss about my wife?"

"Go on," Marcia said.

"It's her music. I miss the music. She'd play the piano for me in the evenings. I'd look forward to her playing. Now I play the piano every once in a while, just so I don't feel so alone. But it's not the same as having her there with me."

As Walter took a sip of water, Marcia saw his hand shaking. She felt her heart swell up with pity for him. He had suffered so much through the loss of his wife, yet he was still trying to go on somehow.

"I don't know why I told you all this."

"We're friends, aren't we?"

"I hope so." Walter met her gaze.

"I'm glad you told me." Marcia again took his hand. Walter smiled, but after a moment, he slowly pulled his hand away. "I've left her piano in the corner of the living room where it was the last time she played it."

They fell silent and Marcia watched Walter consume his beignet, his thoughts on his dead wife. She smiled and tapped her cup. "Hmmm. I love the coffee in this city. It's delicious."

Walter seemed thankful for the change of subject. "Actually, being a bit of a historian, I know the original reason why the coffee in New Orleans was made with chicory."

"Why?" Marcia asked. Already full from one beignet, she pushed the other two toward Walter, who took one and bit into it. She waited while he chewed and swallowed. When Walter finished, he took a sip of water and cleared his throat. "Chicory was put in the coffee because it was cheap and masked the fact that the coffee was diluted."

"I didn't know that."

"I may just have to keep you here in New Orleans a bit longer so I can teach you all you need to know about New Orleans history."

Marcia felt sure her face was on fire. Walter's eyes seemed to penetrate her own. Marcia again thought about kissing him, but pushed the thought away. *He's in mourning for his wife.* Still, she had been too long without a man, and Walter was causing all sorts of mischief inside her. But she turned away and stared down at the notepad. He was obviously not over his wife and she hadn't been on a date in a long time, let alone with a widower. Flirting would have to wait. They were there to solve the mystery of the slave woman.

"I had a visitor last night."

"What happened?"

"The room grew cold, like before, and then, the voice, the moaning. I can't do it justice when I try to describe it. It felt like it was coming from all directions and then suddenly, there she was."

Walter leaned forward, intrigued. "What did she look like?"

"She was very beautiful."

"You could see her clearly?"

"Oh yes. It wasn't what you might think. She wasn't white like a sheet or anything, but light-skinned, with her hair wrapped up in a turban of some sort."

"A tignon."

"What?"

"Chignon or tignon, as they called it in the days of slavery. White women were fearful of their men being seduced by free women of color and quadroons, so they made their men pass a law in the late 1700s which required that all free women of color cover their hair with a turban or tignon."

"Why?"

"White women thought that if their hair was covered, they wouldn't be desirable. It backfired because these women decorated their tignons with fancy jewels or colorful madras cloth."

"So the woman I saw wasn't a slave?"

"That's not for certain. Slave women always had to cover their hair. It's possible, though, that she was a quadroon."

"One thing. Her hands were bound and she was…"

"Go on."

"She was bleeding from a wound in her stomach."

"What kind of wound?"

"Like she had been cut open."

Walter sat back and took a sip of water. "One of Madame LaLaurie's unfortunate victims, I imagine."

"Yes. Oh God, I want to help this woman. I think I might have seen her earlier in the evening, too."

"Where?"

"On the belvedere of the house, near the third floor attic window. Isn't that where…"

"Yes," Walter replied, finishing his coffee. "That's where it all happened. Well, Marcia Watkins, you've got me intrigued. Let's go and see if we can't solve the mystery of this woman and help her find some peace."

Anna shut the door and walked over to lie down on the bed. The house was crowded and she wanted some peace and quiet before the party tonight. Downstairs, Justin and Mrs. St. Jean were busy making last minute arrangements with the caterer and the florist. They expected at least two hundred guests that night for the party and since Mrs. St. Jean was feeling better, she'd insisted on designing the dinner menu herself. After watching her debate between crab cakes and tomato brushetta hors d'oeuvres, Anna had yawned and excused herself in order to take a nap before the party. Besides, both Mrs. St. Jean and Justin were preoccupied and didn't seem to want to hear any of her suggestions for the party.

She closed her eyes and sighed. There had been tension between her and Justin all day. He was angry about her performing on stage the previous night. When they started home, he hardly looked at her and when they got to the house in Vacherie, he had got out and gone inside without waiting for her. She'd let herself in, walked upstairs to her bedroom and gone to sleep, surprised by Justin's behavior.

All at once, she realized how exhausted she was. But as she was just about to fall asleep, the memory of performing on stage returned. Opening her eyes, she smiled. Never before had she felt such exhilaration as when she finished singing and heard the crowd erupt into applause. She'd wanted that feeling to go on forever, but Justin's cold look had instantly killed her euphoria. She remembered Marcia's words of encouragement and sighed. If she wanted to sing, she would lose Justin, of that she was certain. Justin wanted a wife who would accompany him to events and mother his children, not one who was busy with her own career.

Suddenly the bedroom door opened and Justin walked quietly to her bedside. She shut her eyes and pretended to be asleep.

"Anna?"

She did not stir.

"Anna? Are you awake?"

She opened her eyes and looked up at Justin. He smiled down at her and then from behind his back, presented a single long stem red rose.

"For you, my darling."

Anna ignored the rose and turned over on her side, away from him.

"Anna? Are you all right?"

She didn't answer him. She would let him suffer just as he had let her suffer all day. Anna felt the bed shift slightly as Justin sat down besides her. "Anna...I'm sorry I was angry."

She did not stir. Justin reached out and gently touched her shoulder. "Anna, please."

Anna turned over to look at him. "Why were you angry?"

"I felt it was beneath you to take to the stage like that."

"What do you mean, 'beneath me'?"

Justin tried to hand her the rose, but Anna pushed it away. He laid it down on the bedside table. "Must we talk about this now? I'm host of this party tonight and—"

"Yes, we have to talk about it."

Justin stood and ran his hands through his hair, exasperated. "That place is for degenerates. I've told you I never liked it."

Anna sat up. "Why do you call them degenerates?"

"Because they are. They're lower class people. Locals who enjoy nothing more than binging on alcohol and watching a two-bit show while they grope the waitresses. I cringed to think of you working there."

"I know that, Justin, but I liked working there. To tell you the truth, I didn't want to quit."

Justin looked at her in surprise. "What do you mean? Do you propose that after we're married my wife would dare grace the steps of such an establishment?"

"No, I don't. I know you don't want me working there, so that's why I quit. For you."

Justin walked back over to the bed and sat down. "For us, my darling. Don't you see? I'm here to provide for you, to take care of you. You need never think of that horrible place and those awful people again."

"Those 'awful people' are my friends and customers. So if you think that about them, you must think that about me."

"No, my darling, you are above them. It's just you had no choice but to work there, not coming from money."

"You knew I didn't have money when you asked me to be your wife."

"I don't care that you haven't any money."

"Then why did you bring it up just now?"

"I only meant that if you'd had money, I'm certain you wouldn't have ever worked there. You had no choice. But I'm here to provide for you."

Anna stared at Justin. She wanted to tell him off, but all she could think about was losing him and the very thought frightened her. She knew deep down inside she could never find someone like him again. Yet she thought about what Marcia had said about pursuing her dreams. "I know we've never really discussed it, but I like singing. In fact, I've wanted to be a professional singer all my life."

Justin shook his head. "I'm sorry, my darling, I had no idea."

"What if I said that I wanted to try to start a career as a singer? Maybe even call Ed up and try out for Amateur Night?"

Justin suddenly grew angry and reached over, grabbing her arm. "You know I'd never allow that, my darling. You're mine and I'll share you with no one."

Anna tried to pull away. "But I want to sing."

"Then marry someone else."

"Justin—"

"All right, I apologize. I certainly didn't mean that. It's just I want you all to myself. Aren't I enough?"

"Yes, but—"

"Yes but nothing. Come, come, my darling, you're going to have a fantastic life. We'll travel, start a family and live here, in this magnificent home. I will take care of you and you'll never have to worry about money again. What more could a woman want?"

"I—"

Justin grabbed her again, gently this time, and kissed her. "We will have a wonderful life, I promise."

"But Marcia thinks I should try and pursue singing while I'm young—"

Justin pulled away. "I don't know why your sister came here if she's only going to encourage you to do something that I'm certain you will fail at."

"I have talent."

Justin smiled sarcastically at her.

"I do. Everyone thought so last night."

"They were just being kind at your good-bye party."

Anna glared at him. "How can you be so cruel?"

"I'm not trying to be cruel. I'm trying to be honest. Your singing was all right, but you're no great talent, Anna."

"I have enough talent. Maybe even enough to get a record contract."

Justin shook his head, laughing at her. "Many people think that and end up being cocktail waitresses."

Anna shook her head. "You knew I was a cocktail waitress. It never seemed to bother you before."

"It doesn't. Mother loves you. She thinks you'll make a good wife and mother. That's all that's important. Frankly, if I'd wanted a career woman, I would have gone for someone with an education."

His words stung her and she got out of bed. "Thanks, Justin. I feel so much better now."

Justin took off his jacket and walking up behind her, wrapped his arms around her waist and gently kissed her neck.

"Come, darling, no more arguments, hmm? Let's make up."

Anna pulled away.

"Will you deny me?"

"Oh, Justin, how can I think of making love when I'm not sure you even respect me?"

Justin turned her around to face him. "I'm marrying you, not a career woman. I'll be honest, darling. If I'd wanted a woman with a career, I could have had that a long time ago. You bring nothing to this marriage but your youth and beauty and that's what I want. I love you. No more discussion of singing or else I'll—"

Anna turned away from him. Justin sighed and she heard him putting his jacket on behind her. "I'd better go and see how Mother's getting on. Take a rest, darling. You look exhausted. Make sure and wear the blue velvet dress I bought you. It looks stunning."

Anna didn't say anything as she heard the door open and shut behind Justin. She stared down at the diamond ring on her hand and shook her head. She loved Justin, but he wanted things his own way. But he was right. Starting a career in music was a big risk. Most people failed. If she married Justin, she'd never have to worry again and worry was something she never wanted to do again.

After finishing their coffees, Marcia and Walter got into Walter's car and drove over to the Jefferson Parish Library branch in Gretna. Along the way, they chatted about Marcia's trip, trying to keep their minds off the slave woman for at least a while.

"Have you seen any of the tourist sights?"

"I've just been around the French Quarter and the Garden District."

"Pretty there, isn't it?"

"Anna pointed out Anne Rice's house. It's so big! And the property is so well-maintained."

"Her home is a big tourist attraction. Did you ride the St. Charles streetcar?"

"I did. I could ride along St. Charles Avenue all day. I love all the magnificent homes with their manicured lawns. Some of the houses even had Greek columns."

Walter laughed. "There was a time when having a Greek Revival home was all the rage."

"They're nice, but I wouldn't want to live in one. I'd feel like the lady of the manor."

Walter laughed. "I know what you mean." He turned to look at her. "When's your sister getting married?"

"Next week."

"That's soon, isn't it?"

"Too soon, if you ask me," Marcia said before she could stop herself. When she saw Walter's look of surprise, she wanted to kick herself. "I'm sorry, I shouldn't have said that."

"That's all right. It's none of my business."

They fell silent for a moment. Marcia stared out the window. "I'm worried."

"About what?"

"Anna. It's just been such a whirlwind romance, and I hardly know Justin at all. I think she's entering into marriage too lightly." *And for all the wrong reasons.*

Walter turned off the highway into Gretna. "Don't worry. Justin St. Jean has been down this road before. That's just the way Justin is. He was like that with Beatrice. They were married after only two months' courtship. It's a shame it didn't work out. They seemed genuinely in love."

Marcia looked at him in surprise. "What do you mean, 'didn't work out'? She died of cancer."

Walter looked over at her. "No, she left him, about a year ago, I believe."

"Justin said that she died of cancer a few years ago. Wait a minute, I think he said her name was Tiffany."

"Maybe he was married to someone else who I never met. But he brought Beatrice around everywhere he went. They were married two years ago in St. Louis Cathedral. She's from one of New Orleans' richest families…"

Marcia was only half-listening. *Why did Justin lie to me? Does Anna know about his ex-wife?*

"Beatrice was friendly. Flo had just died and she was kind to me."

Justin had been married twice before? The image of him as a widower who'd finally found love with her sister disappeared from her mind. "Do you know how they met?"

"I think she told me they met at a Mardi Gras party at Justin's plantation home. She's a very nice woman, but not very educated. She liked parties, mostly, and shopping. Her parents had sent her to several private schools in Europe, but she never finished school. She and Justin were married soon after her eighteenth birthday."

He likes them young, doesn't he?

"She stayed at the apartment at LaLaurie Mansion a few times."

"She did?"

"Yes, she liked it there. She once told me that she'd pretend that she was the mistress of the house. I guess she was just a kid really."

"Does this woman…"

"Beatrice Beauregard, like the famous landmark in the French Quarter."

"Does she still live in New Orleans?"

"I don't know. Her parents still live in the Garden District." Walter turned to look at her again. "I know what you're thinking, but it's no big secret that Justin's been hiding from you. Everyone knew of his marriage to Beatrice Beauregard. I'm sure your sister knows and it's all just a misunderstanding."

Marcia nodded her head, but she wasn't as certain as Walter. She needed to talk to Anna, but knew that with the party tonight, the timing wasn't right. If Anna didn't know, she didn't want to upset her sister in front of strangers. Perhaps tomorrow, she thought. Either way, she had to know if Anna knew about Beatrice.

"Now, here we are," he said as they drove into a spot in the library's parking lot.

***

"So what's the news on that property, Albert?"

Justin was upstairs in his home office, talking on the phone with his lawyer, Albert Stewart.

"It's owned by Morgan Realty. They have five tenants, four rental apartments and the Louis Armstrong," Albert said.

"What are the chances of making an outright purchase?"

"Pretty good. The building is in need of repairs, which should lower the price, although the Louis Armstrong has been making a steady profit."

"No matter. I plan on tearing it down and turning the whole building into private apartments."

"That'd be a shame. Big loss of revenue. Besides, I'm just not sure why you want to invest in this building. You're already in over your head with other investment deals and the finances are stretched thin."

"It's my business why I want to buy the building, all right? You're my lawyer, not my financial advisor. All you need to do is draw up the papers and collect your fee, or I'll find myself another lawyer, understand?"

"Yes sir, I do. I'll have them for you by early next week."

"Monday morning, I want them by Monday morning."

"But it's the weekend and—"

"So charge me more. And make sure you have those other papers ready for Anna to sign. I want them ready by Monday, too."

"Okay, Justin. It's going to cost you extra to—"

"Just do it."

Justin hung up the phone and leaned back in the leather office chair. He could murder that idiot manager at the Louis Armstrong for bringing Anna up on stage and encouraging her. He wanted Anna all to himself and he'd done the one thing that stood in the way of having Anna all to himself. The Louis Armstrong would soon just be a memory.

An hour later, Marcia and Walter were surrounded by books on New Orleans history. She felt her head spinning. While Walter went to use the microfiche, Marcia went to the ladies' room to splash cold water on her face. As she dried her face with a paper towel, Justin St. Jean filled her mind. *Why would he lie?* She emerged from the restroom and found Walter hard at work reading through the microfiche of the *New Orleans Bee*.

"Find anything yet?"

"Not yet. Don't worry, this might take some time, but we'll find what we're looking for."

Marcia looked over at the huge pile of books on the table and then over at the reference desk.

"I'm going to take a break from this and see if I can get help from the librarian."

Marcia went to the front and asked the librarian for information regarding Madame LaLaurie. The librarian searched for a while in a back room and came back with a scrapbook labeled IMPORTANT EVENTS—1830–1840.

"You see, it was a big story back then. The way those slaves were killed was just horrible."

"Can I take this to the other room to examine it?"

"Of course you can," the librarian said. "Just be sure to return it to me before you leave."

Marcia carried the heavy book over to the table and began to look through the various articles. After about half an hour, she heard Walter calling her.

"Hey, got something here."

Marcia hurried over and stood behind Walter, very aware of his fragrant aftershave, as he scrolled through to the right page of the microfiche.

"Here we are."

The page he pulled up was a newspaper article in the *New Orleans Bee* dated April 12, 1834.

"It's further down, kind of hard to read without straining your eyes, but it's all there. Come, I'll pull up a chair so you can see better."

Walter stood and pulled a chair next to him, patted it, and smiled at Marcia. Marcia felt her breath catch at the back of her throat at his smile. When he smiled, his whole face lit up. She sat down and leaned in toward Walter so she could see the screen better.

Half of the newspaper was in French and the other half in English. Marcia's eyes scanned to a headline on the lower half of the page:

LALAURIE MANSION DESTROYED IN FIRE; SLAVES FOUND MURDERED

Down below, although it was hard to make out, was the description of the fire and the subsequent destruction of the home:

"…eleven slaves more or less horribly mutilated, suspended by the neck with their limbs apparently stretched or torn from one extremity to the other. Enraged neighbors stormed the fire-damaged house, throwing furniture into the street and shredding valuable paintings and documents. The LaLauries have made good their escape and have yet to be seen in these parts."

"So the neighbors destroyed the house after they fled."

"Appears so. I guess when you get a lynch mob together and there's no one to lynch, they go after the next best thing."

"What about the slaves? It doesn't say anything about the slaves that were rescued from the home."

Walter shook his head. "No. Nothing. The ones that were still alive were auctioned off that week, I suppose."

"Can you print out this article?"

Walter stood up. "I don't know how, but I'll go and ask the librarian."

Heavy-hearted, Marcia stared at the screen as Walter walked to the reference desk. How could human beings treat other human beings that way? Didn't they have any conscience at all? Then, after going through hell, the survivors had been simply auctioned off to someone else. God only knew what had become of them. She sat back in her chair and sighed. Finding any information about the slave woman was going to be far more difficult than she'd anticipated. In all likelihood the woman had died in the house, but when? Did Madame LaLaurie kill her? Was "Sam" her child or a spouse who had been auctioned off? They would have to find bills of sale or, and she cringed at this thought, "ownership" papers to have any hope of uncovering the identity of the slave woman and her mysterious "Sam."

Walter returned a minute later with a printout of the article.

"Here we go. Not the greatest copy, but the best we're going to get."

"What now?"

Walter sat back down. "I know it's frustrating, but we'll find something."

"I've got only a week to help this woman."

"Don't worry. We're making progress." Walter touched her arm and when Marcia looked over at him, she felt a tingling sensation travel through of her body. *What's happening to me? I don't even know this man.*

Walter was looking at her with a small smile. "I think it's wonderful you want to help. Now, back to work. We haven't much more time today. See if you can't find something in that big scrapbook over there. Anything would be helpful."

"All right."

She went back to the table and looked through the scrapbook. Toward the middle of the book, in the section marked 1833, she found an article that intrigued her. "Hey, something interesting here."

"What is it?" Walter asked.

"When I was walking through Pirate's Alley the other day, I thought I felt someone watching me. When I turned around, there was no one there. But it was weird. I *knew* someone was watching me."

"You're not trying to suggest Pirate's Alley is haunted?"

"No, just that I got a strange feeling. According to this article, dated March 5, 1833, 'a negro man was found dead, his throat slashed on the deep side of Pirate's Alley.'"

She turned to Walter. "Found dead? But not murdered?"

"Just the language of the time. Besides, slaves were property. Go on."

"Here's the interesting part. 'The negro belonging to Dr. LaLaurie had been a runaway for two days before he was discovered in the alley.'"

Walter shook his head. "Does the article give the name of the man?"

"No, not here."

"There has to be a record of it somewhere. His throat was slashed. It had to be murder." She shut the scrapbook and glanced down at her watch. "It's frustrating to stop now, but I have to get ready for the party tonight at the St. Jeans'."

Walter whistled under his breath. "Fancy. Fine house out there in Vacherie. On the River Road."

"River Road?"

"The road leading from New Orleans to Baton Rouge. It's where all the old plantation homes once stood, although most of them were destroyed during the Civil War when the Union soldiers shelled the homes along the Mississippi. The St. Jeans have owned that house nearly two hundred years."

"We made a little progress in our research today," Marcia said as they walked out of the library and toward Walter's car. "Maybe we can meet tomorrow?" She wanted to find out who Sam was, but she also wanted to see Walter again.

"All right, maybe tomorrow afternoon. Let's get going. We don't want to make you late to Mr. St. Jean's party."

CHAPTER EIGHT

Justin sent Marcus to pick Marcia up at seven o'clock that evening for the party. With her hair up and a fresh manicure, she emerged from the mansion in a black strapless dress and matching heels.

Though Marcia tried to keep her mind focused on making a good impression on Justin's friends and family, for Anna's sake, she couldn't help thinking of what Walter had told her about Beatrice. Why had the marriage been so short-lived? Maybe Justin had been married more than two times. How many more women had there been in his life? Maybe, and this was what frightened her, Justin wasn't really in love with Anna.

Marcus helped her into the car and as they headed out of the French Quarter, she sighed. *Anna and Justin say they knew they were meant for one another in just two months, so maybe love at first sight really does happen.* But as she thought about them, a nagging worry returned. Justin St. Jean was not being completely honest with her sister. Though she had less than a week, Marcia resolved to make sure that her sister wasn't throwing her life and dreams away for a man who wasn't completely trustworthy or deserving.

As the car made its way toward Vacherie, Marcia leaned forward.

"I hear the River Road has many beautiful plantation homes."

"It sure does, ma'am. Do you know anything about plantation life?"

"Only what I've seen in *Gone with the Wind.*"

Marcus laughed. "That was Georgia, but some things are the same. White folks had fancy parties in grand ballrooms and sat on the porch sipping mint juleps while slaves did the work that needed to get done. And they worked hard, especially the field hands who worked from sun up to sun down with little food and not much else."

"I find it hard to believe that slave owners would treat people so badly. If slaves were property, didn't they want to keep them around for as long as possible?" Marcia asked.

"Slaves weren't as expensive as you might think. Planting sugar and tobacco and harvesting it was real back-breaking work, especially in the summertime in New Orleans. You're lucky you're here in the fall, 'cause in the summer it's too much even to lift a glass of water to your mouth, the heat and humidity is so bad. Try to imagine laboring all day in horrible heat and humidity with nothing to keep you going except some vegetables you've grown for yourself. No, ma'am, slaves didn't live long at all. You were an old man at thirty and most died young. But the slave owner's mentality was to buy you young, work you till you died in ten, twelve years, and then get another to replace you. It was cheaper that way, in their minds, than feeding and clothing you properly."

As Marcus took the next exit, he nodded toward the Mississippi River.

"Old Man River here was a big draw for planters. They built their homes on the road that ran parallel to the river, the Great River Road we're on right now. During the Civil War, the Yankees shelled plantation homes all along the river, destroying most of them."

"Not all of them?"

"No, the homes of citizens who signed an oath of allegiance to the United States of America were spared. The St. Jeans did that."

"What is an oath of allegiance?"

"Meaning you pledged to honor the laws of the United States of America, not those of the Confederacy. It's a shame, though, 'cause even the homes that did survive the war were torn down and replaced by factories, and recently, chemical plants."

Gazing out the window, Marcia could see several ugly-looking chemical factories leaking fumes and smoke into the sky.

"That is a shame."

"The River Road used to be one of the most beautiful roads in the South, tree-lined and with a clear view of the Mississippi as you made your way by horse drawn carriage or just sat on the porch of one of those fine plantation houses."

"The homes were like the one in *Gone with the Wind*?"

Marcus laughed, shaking his head. "Oh, no, not at all. There are just two that look like that—the St. Jean home and a place called Nottoway. They were built in the Greek Revival style of the time."

"Greek Revival? I know, white with sweeping columns and wrap-around porches."

"That's right. Nottoway is the largest plantation home in the South. It was given that name because when construction crews were given the design for the home by the architect, they shook their heads and said, 'There's not a way that home can be built.'"

Marcia laughed. "That's funny. Is it true?"

"Yes, ma'am, it is. It was a great construction project for the time."

"You know so much about these homes. But what about the slaves that worked the plantations? Do you know anything about them?"

"Not too much. Slaves were given Christian names, like Isaiah or Earl or Sam…"

The name caused Marcia's head to pop up. "Sam?"

"Sure, it was a common name. Most slaves went by only their first names and if they did have a last name, it was their master's last name. So a slave belonging to a Mr. Pugh was Thomas Pugh."

"What about records?"

"Slave records, you mean?"

"Right."

"I think slaves were listed by their first name and general description, mulatto or negro or short or fat, etc. If slaves were inherited property after the death of the plantation owner, they were listed, just like I described, in a log, along with the pigs, the house, the machinery, etc."

"It would be hard to track the whereabouts of one slave?"

"It sure would. There weren't even proper birth and death records kept. Most slaves had to approximate their age. Most owners didn't keep accurate records when it came to selling off one of their slaves."

"What about slaves that were set free?"

"Happened often enough. Either your master got a conscience or didn't need you anymore or you bought your own freedom. Lots of slaves did that. Manumissions, they were called."

"What about those records?"

"I'm sure they're around somewhere, I just wouldn't know where."

"How come you know so much about slavery, Marcus?"

"My family's been in Louisiana for more than two hundred years."

"Do you know where your ancestors originally came from?"

"Senegal."

"What about other slaves that arrived in Louisiana, where did they come from?"

"Most came from the Caribbean, West Indies, and others straight from Africa."

Marcia sat back, discouraged for the moment. If Madame LaLaurie had purchased the slave woman and brought her to live at the mansion, it was going to be difficult to determine the woman's real identity. She cringed as she thought of the number of slaves who might have had the first name Sam, if Sam were indeed a slave, which she assumed he was.

"We're almost there," Marcus said, interrupting her thoughts. "On the right, at 13034, is the Destrehan plantation. It was built in the 1780s by a free man of color."

"A free man of color? You mean a black man owned this?"

"Sure. They were referred to as mulattoes or colored and they could own land and slaves, which many of them did."

"Were they free to do as they pleased?"

"Sure, for the most part. Free men of color could even pick mistresses at quadroon balls and such."

This perked Marcia's interest. "Quadroon balls? Like in the French Quarter?"

"Right. Creoles, whites, and free men of color, meaning mixed races, could go there and pick mistresses from amongst the mulatto and quadroon women there."

Marcus slowed the car and made a right turn down a long drive.

"Here we are. 2642 River Road. The St. Jean Plantation Home."

"My, oh my," Marcia said. Before her stood the most magnificent home she had ever seen. White columns and a broad wraparound porch indicated the already familiar Greek Revival style. A great lawn and garden stretched out before her as Marcus drove the car into a circular driveway.

"My God. I had no idea that his home would be so grand," Marcia said.

"I know. Everyone thinks that when they first see this place. There are stables in the back and a year ago, about the time Mr. St. Jean was killed, they tore down some old slave quarters to build a pool house."

"Slave quarters?"

"Yup. Back of the house there used to sit twenty-two slave cabins. Now there's only a handful left, used mostly for storage."

"Did you say that Mr. St. Jean was killed?"

"He fell through some floorboards when he was inspecting the construction of the pool house. Tragic accident. Now I better let you out so you can join the party."

Marcus came around to open the door for her. Marcia took his gloved hand when he offered it to her. He helped her out and shut the door behind her. "I'll be here waiting for you when you come out. Have a good time."

"Thanks, Marcus," Marcia said as she made her way toward the front door. She suddenly felt nervous and wished that she had asked Walter to come with her. She rang the bell and a black man dressed in tails opened the door.

"Good evening, madam."

"Good evening."

"Please do come in."

Marcia stepped into the gilded marble hallway and gasped at the opulence of the crystal chandeliers and the elegant curved staircase.

"May I take your wrap?"

She nodded and removed her shawl and handed it to him. He hung it in a closet nearby and turning, bowed deeply. "I am Evers, the butler."

"Marcia Watkins."

"It is a pleasure to meet you, Ms. Watkins. You have been anxiously awaited. May I escort you to the ballroom?"

"Yes, thank you."

Marcia followed the butler to the grand ballroom at the end of a long hallway. Along the walls were old portraits of men and women.

"Who are these people on the walls?"

"They are the former owners of the home, the ancestors of the St. Jeans."

One of the portraits caught her eye and she paused for a moment to take a closer look. It was of a man in his fifties, distinguished-looking with graying hair and heavy sideburns. The man's clothes and hairstyle indicated the 1800s. Something in the deep blue of his eyes caught her attention. She felt disturbed, off balance for a moment, and tried to steady herself.

Stopping, Evers looked back at her. "Are you all right, madam?"

"Yes, Evers. Can you tell me who this man is here?"

Evers walked back to her and stood in front of the portrait. "Ah yes, that is Matthew Abernathy. He was the owner of this plantation and a distant relation of Mr. St. Jean, by marriage, I believe. This portrait was painted in 1834, a few months before his death."

"Do you know how he died?"

"Natural causes, as far as I know. Shall we continue to the ballroom?"

"Yes, sorry, Evers."

"No problem at all, madam."

As they continued down the hallway to the ballroom, Marcia could hear the hum of voices and the clinking of glasses. When Evers opened the double doors into the ballroom, Marcia again gasped. The ballroom was as grand a room as she had ever seen. There were crystal chandeliers lining the ceiling and white marble statuary. Elegantly dressed gentlemen in black tuxedos and women dressed in long evening dresses filled the large space. Waiters passed among them with trays of appetizers and alongside one wall was a mahogany bar where two bartenders attended to the guests. Entering the room, Marcia could feel many pairs of eyes turning to her. She felt a little nervous and out of place, especially when she couldn't see Justin or Anna anywhere. She walked to the bar and ordered a glass of wine.

While she waited for the bartender to pour her drink, she surveyed the crowd. Her heart sank when she saw that almost everyone had brought a date. It seemed as if she were the only single woman there. Usually at such affairs, she would stand by the bar, smile and "make herself available," hoping that any single man there would approach her, but tonight, for some reason, she had no interest in doing that. *There's no one as sexy as Walter.* A thought suddenly occurred to her. Around Walter, she felt as if she could be herself. She was still nervous, as she was so attracted to him, but he didn't make her feel that she was boring or rambling on incessantly about nothing. She could talk to him. She recalled their conversation in the car and a smile formed on her lips. He made her weak in the knees every time he smiled at her. A pleasant chill coursed through her body as she recalled sitting close to him and inhaling his enticing aftershave.

"Here's your wine, ma'am."

She snapped back to reality and took the glass the bartender handed her. "Thank you."

She sipped the wine, feeling strangely warm, although the room was airy and cool. Walter had been a good sport to accompany her on her ghost hunt. *Why did he participate? What does he think of me?* Regardless, he had taken the time out of his day to help her and she realized that she had not properly thanked him, so caught up was she in the information they had uncovered about LaLaurie Mansion. *After the party tonight, if it's not too late, I'll go over and thank him.*

Just then, an elegant older woman with a head full of blondish-gray hair approached her in a wheelchair. She gave Marcia the once-over and then nodded her head in greeting.

"Ms. Watkins?"

"Yes?"

"I'm Josephine St. Jean, Justin's mother."

"Oh, a pleasure to meet you, Mrs. St. Jean." Marcia leaned down and shook Mrs. St. Jean's hand. For a supposedly sick woman, her handshake was firm.

"Find the place all right?"

"Yes, Justin sent the car."

"Ah, yes, Marcus. I hope that boy didn't talk your ear off."

"No."

"Those boys just don't know when to shut up. It's just natural to talk with his people."

Marcia stared at Mrs. St. Jean, unable to hide the shock in her face.

"I didn't mean you, dear. I just meant it's so hard to get good help these days."

"Uh-huh."

"You don't really look like your sister. She's a lovely girl."

Marcia didn't know how to take that comment either so she just smiled. *Mrs. St. Jean isn't shy about speaking her mind.*

"I like her. She's quiet and doesn't cause a fuss. She'll make a fine wife for Justin. Well, come on in and join the party. I don't know where Justin got off to, but he's around here somewhere."

Before Marcia could respond, Mrs. St. Jean had steered her wheelchair over to another couple. As Marcia took another sip of wine, she caught sight of Justin and Anna in the corner of the room and waved. Anna walked over, dressed in a floor length velvet cocktail dress that accentuated her curves and coloring. Although she looked stunning, Marcia had a sixth sense that something was not quite right with her.

"You look so beautiful."

"Thanks," Anna said as they hugged. "Justin bought me the dress."

"Very nice." Marcia was dying to talk to Anna alone, but knew now was not the right time. "Is everything all right?"

"Fine," Anna said, looking uncomfortable for a moment. "I'm just a little tired. I tried to have a nap earlier, but I really couldn't sleep. I'll be okay. You look great, by the way. There are some eligible men here tonight," Anna said, looking around the room. "Should I introduce you?"

"Thanks, but no thanks. I'm here for you."

Anna took her hand and squeezed. Marcia felt her clammy hand and frowned. "Are you sure you're all right?"

"Fine. There's just so many people here and they all want to meet me and well, it's a lot of work."

"You're doing fine. And I've already told you how stunning you look. Don't be nervous."

"Thanks. What would I do without you?"

Marcia leaned in to Anna. "Anna, do you think we might have some time later to talk? I—"

Anna appeared not to have heard her. "Have you met Mrs. St. Jean?"

"Yes, I have."

Anna laughed. "She comes off as kind of standoffish, but she's nice when you get to know her."

"I'm surprised to see her here. I thought she was gravely ill."

"She is, but she's a Southern woman, and Southern women are the ultimate hostesses. As the woman of the house, she had to make an appearance."

Marcia took a sip of wine as Anna stopped a passing waiter to grab a couple of shrimp hors d' oeuvres. She took a bite of hers and handed one to Marcia, who devoured it. She hadn't had anything to eat since breakfast and was famished.

"It is a beautiful house. I guess, though *house* isn't the appropriate word."

"I know. It used to be a sugar plantation. The cabins in the back which are used for storage and such, used to be slave cabins."

"Doesn't that kind of give you the creeps?"

Anna shrugged. "It was long ago."

"Listen, Anna. Did you and Justin…?"

Just at that moment, two little boys dressed in dark suits ran through the door, followed by a frazzled-looking nanny. They began to laugh and chase one another around the bar and almost crashed into a waiter who was carrying a tray of champagne flutes. Marcia saw Justin watching the melee with a look of horror on his face. After a moment, that look changed to anger. He quickly walked over to a gentleman, a younger version of himself, with black hair and the same coloring.

"Who is that man?"

"Who? Oh, that's Justin's younger brother, Stephen. The boys are his. They are so naughty, and their mother, Tina, is useless," Anna said, pointing to an attractive blond woman in a tight red cocktail dress. She was standing at the bar, taking a tequila shot and swaying a bit. Marcia could see that she was drunk.

"Is she…?" Marcia began.

"Yup. Always. I tried to get to know her, but she didn't have any time for me. She looks down her nose at me and one time at dinner and in front of everyone, told Justin that if he had kids with me, it was a toss of a coin what color they'd come out."

"Oh my God."

"Justin just about hit her. He ordered Stephen to escort her out, which he did. I heard them arguing later."

"What were they arguing about?"

Anna took another bite of her shrimp. "About how Stephen had to learn to control her better. How he had to watch her and make sure she didn't embarrass the family."

Marcia didn't like the sound of that. Not only was Justin trying to control Anna, but his brother as well. "What did Stephen say?"

"He told him that he couldn't. That Tina wouldn't listen to him. I don't know why Stephen married her."

"She's quite beautiful, if you go for the bleached blond tart look."

"Yeah, she was her high school prom queen. I don't think she ever loved Stephen. She just wanted the good life."

Tina swayed again, almost spilling her drink, but a man standing next to her grabbed her arm, steadying her. She laughed and took an exaggerated gulp of her drink. Anna shook her head. "It's embarrassing, but she's a drunk. What can you do?"

"Did she ever apologize for what she said about you?"

"The whole family did. They said they don't think that way and they were happy Justin was marrying me. She gave me sort of an apology afterwards, but I knew she didn't mean it. I know she didn't mean what she said either. She's just bored, I guess. She doesn't have anything to do all day but shop."

"And the kids?"

"You can see for yourself."

"Did she ever want them, do you think?"

"Probably not. She's not much of a mother to them."

"The nanny doesn't seem to be doing that good of a job either," Marcia said as they watched the nanny go from one end of the room to the other trying to round up the kids. Justin was speaking angrily to Stephen and pointing emphatically at the kids.

"Tina's family has money. Justin told me that they are 'new money' and she married Stephen for the St. Jean name and connections. She hasn't done much since the marriage except breed. That's enough, though, to secure her brother's position."

"What do you mean?"

"That's partly the reason Justin wants kids. When his mother passes on, this house and land will go to him. But when he dies, if he doesn't have an heir, it will all go to his brother, and well, Tina and the children."

"Is that why Justin is in such a rush to start a family?"

Anna laughed. "Oh, no. I know what you're thinking, but Justin loves kids. Wants a whole houseful of them. Always has."

At that moment, Justin hurried over to the nanny with Stephen in tow. "Edna. I thought I told you to keep those boys out of here."

"I'm sorry, Mr. St. Jean, but—"

"Just get these damn kids out of here! Now!"

Conversation stopped as people turned to see what all the commotion was about. Justin walked over to one of the little boys and grabbing his arm, pulled him off the floor and toward the door. "Lionel, I thought I told you to keep out of this room. Get out now!"

"Ow! That hurts!" The boy tried to pull away, but Justin pulled him to the door, followed by Stephen, the other boy and Edna, the nanny, who wrung her hands in nervousness.

Marcia was shocked by Justin's behavior. It certainly wasn't what she expected from someone who was so desperate to have children, and right away. *He doesn't have any patience at all.* What Anna said about having an heir leapt into her mind. Now she was more concerned than ever that Justin St. Jean was simply looking for an heir and not a wife to love.

Anna turned to her. "Come on. Let me show you the gardens before dinner."

They both grabbed a glass of champagne off a tray and went out a pair of French doors and into the well-tended garden outside.

"What a magnificent garden."

"Yeah, it's beautiful. I love to come out here when I'm staying here."

"Anna, I want to talk to you."

"About what?"

Marcia took a sip of her drink for courage and looked at Anna. "I was talking to Walter Dufrane…"

"Oh, you two met? I didn't know that. He's a handsome man, isn't he? Kind of a recluse though."

Marcia felt her cheeks grow warm, but she continued on. "He is, but he's actually quite nice. Anyway, like I was saying, Walter said that Justin was married to someone else, maybe someone after Tiffany. A Beatrice—"

"Beauregard."

"You know."

Anna took a sip of her drink. "Of course I know. They were married for only a year. It didn't work out."

"Oh. Do you know why?"

"No," Anna said, looking at Marcia. "It wasn't any of my business."

"Your future husband's past is not your business?"

"No. And like you just said, it's the past. Justin doesn't know about all of my old boyfriends."

"You weren't married to any of them."

"What's your point?"

"There shouldn't be such secrecy between you two, that's all I'm saying."

"It's not a secret. He told me that they just couldn't get along."

"How long were they together before they got married?"

"Not long. A couple of months."

"Do you see a pattern emerging here?"

"Stop it, Marcia."

"Stop what?"

"Stop being so suspicious."

"I can't help it. Your future husband's been married twice before."

"Why are you judging him? His wife died and he met someone soon after. Beatrice just wasn't right for him. I am."

"Why didn't he mention Beatrice at dinner?"

"Why should he?"

"He mentioned Tiffany."

"He really loved her."

"But not Beatrice?"

"What's your point, Marcia?"

"How do you know he really loves you? His mother seems to think you'd make a good wife and mother. Is he marrying you just so he can have kids?"

Anna turned to her. "I'm only going to say this one last time. I've made up my mind. I'm marrying Justin. I want children as well, all right? You're supposed to be here to support me and all you've done is question my love for Justin and his for me."

"I've done no such thing. I've only questioned the rush to marry and the urgency to start a family right away. He's so much older—"

"He's only forty-six."

"Only? He and I should be dating."

"Stop it, Marcia, or I'm going to go back inside."

Marcia grabbed Anna's arm. "All right, we'll drop it. I just wanted to make sure you knew about Beatrice."

"I do." Anna took another sip of her drink. "We'd better get back before Justin starts to wonder where we've gone."

It was obvious Justin was angry when they reappeared in the ball-room. Marcia could tell by the way he took Anna's arm to escort her into dinner. He whispered something angrily into her ear and seemed doubly upset when he discovered they had been in the gardens without his permission. All through dinner, Marcia noticed he kept his hand on Anna's and from time to time, he gave her a hard stare. Other than that, he did his best to ignore Marcia. *So much for getting to know one another better.* When she did get a moment to speak with him, he turned away. Though Marcia kept a smile on her face, inside she was seething. Justin St. Jean had no interest in knowing her. The only thing he wanted was Anna.

She tried to continue with the pleasantries throughout the evening, but what she really wanted was to go back to the apartment and talk with Walter. Although Justin's friends were polite, she found them distant and very pretentious. During dinner the talk had been of investments and business affairs and after dinner, the men retired for cigars and brandy while the women were left behind to chat about the latest fashions over coffee with cake. All the women gushed about Anna's wedding, and Marcia listened to their chatter until she felt she could make her excuses and go back to town.

Anna walked her to the door as Justin was engaged with his friends. "Tomorrow we're going to church. Do you want to come with us?"

"Uh, no. I want to stay in and rest."

"All right. I'll drop by around two and we'll go shopping for dresses."

"Will any shops be open? It's Sunday."

"Sure. The malls are open. I'll see you then."

"Okay. It's a date." As Marcia hugged Anna good-bye, she felt guilty for bringing up Beatrice. She knew she should be happy for her sister, and accept Justin for who he was, but she just couldn't shake the feeling that he wasn't right for Anna. She didn't trust him. But she smiled at Anna and gave her another hug. "I'm happy for you. Let's just focus on getting you a beautiful dress. Rest and don't worry about anything. The wedding's going to be wonderful."

"I know. I know it will be."

CHAPTER NINE

Walter sat at the piano trying to concentrate. From time to time, he would glance over at the picture of Flo. *Come on, concentrate.* He was working on a new piece, a jazz piece, but each time his hands touched the keys, he would lose his train of thought and have to start over. He'd been sitting at the piano since after lunch, but had done very little. Something was bothering him. He knew what it was and was trying to force the feeling away, but he couldn't. He felt guilty.

You're a liar, his conscience accused. He didn't know why he'd told Marcia that he played only to be close to Flo. He loved playing the piano. In fact, it gave him life. Playing the piano was the only reason he had for getting up in the mornings, and although it sounded romantic to say he played for Flo, he played for himself, always had and always would.

At the same time, he couldn't get Marcia off his mind. He didn't know why she was interested in helping a ghost, but he was intrigued by her goodness, by her desire to do all she could to help the slave woman find "Sam." She certainly had nothing to gain by helping the woman, but that didn't seem to even be a consideration for her. Such kindness was rare to find in a person nowadays.

He got up and helped himself to a glass of lemonade in the kitchen. He wasn't sure why, but as he drank down the cool liquid, he thought about Flo's Joint. *I wonder if anyone's bought the place yet. It's been two years…I'm sure they have.* Flo's Joint was located in the basement of a building right in the French Quarter on North Rampart Street. He hadn't been by there in two years. It was strange to think about Flo's Joint when he hadn't in such a long time. At the same time, Marcia's face flashed before him. He didn't know why there was a connection between her and Flo's Joint, but since meeting her, he was beginning to think a lot about his music and of opening a jazz club. *Marcia Watkins.* He recalled sitting next to her, so close that they almost touched, so close that the fragrance of her perfume hung in the air of his car. What was it about her that kept coming back to him? Why was her presence interrupting his life?

On the ride back to LaLaurie Mansion, Marcia couldn't stop thinking about Anna and Justin. Did he love her sister? Or did he love only her youth and beauty? Given their conversation tonight, it seemed Anna was determined to marry Justin, no matter what. She'd completely forgotten to ask Anna if she'd talked to Justin about pursuing her singing career, but made a mental note to ask her tomorrow.

As they drove into the French Quarter, an excited feeling came over Marcia but she didn't know why. Then she remembered that she was going to see Walter in a few minutes to thank him for helping her today. She hurriedly opened her purse and got out her compact to check her makeup. As she removed her lipstick, her hand went instinctively to her lips. She wondered what it would feel like to kiss Walter. His lips looked so soft and alluring. She leaned her head back against the seat and shut her eyes, allowing herself to daydream about him.

"Marcia..."

He walked toward her, and began to undress her. She moaned as he kissed her neck and gently caressed her shoulders. Her dress fell to the floor and he picked her up, ever so gently, and carried her to the bed. He kissed her all along her body, starting with her throat, and stopping at her breasts. He took one nipple into his mouth and suckled, while he spread her open and kneaded her most intimate...

"Here we are, Ms. Watkins," Marcus said, snapping her out of her dream.

She opened her eyes. *Darn...just a dream.* "Thanks, Marcus."

Marcus got out and opened the door for her.

"Have a good night."

"Thank you, Marcus. Take care."

As she turned to go inside, she suddenly saw the woman who worked at the Bourbon Orleans standing on the corner beneath a street lamp, waving at her. She waved back. Marcus looked at Marcia and then over to where the woman stood before turning back to Marcia with a strange look on his face.

"Who are you waving to, Ms. Watkins?"

"That woman. Across the street. I met her the other day. She works at the Bourbon Orleans."

Marcus looked where she pointed and then back at her with a strange look. "What woman?"

"The one there, beneath the street lamp."

Marcus again looked over at the street lamp before shaking his head. "I don't see her."

"She's right…"

But just as the words were out of her mouth, she suddenly didn't see the woman anymore. Strange, she thought. *She was just there.*

"Never mind. I must be tired. Good night."

"Good night again, ma'am," Marcus said as he got into the limousine.

Determined to talk to Walter, she climbed the marble steps, unlocked the front door, and stepped inside the foyer. It was dark and she was suddenly frightened. Looking around, she hurried toward the stairway and dashed up the stairs as fast as her feet could carry her. As she rounded the corner to enter the hallway, she paused, her breath heavy. She was afraid, so afraid of seeing *something. All I have to do is get to Walter's door and pray he's still awake.* She glanced down at her watch and saw that it was close to ten o'clock. She peeked around the corner again and saw nothing but a dark hallway. Although her logical side told her she was being silly, she could not allay her fear of seeing the ghost. She took a deep breath and then looking straight ahead, rounded the corner and made a run for Walter's door. She knocked, and almost immediately the door was opened. Seeing Walter dressed in a pair of blue sweats made her sigh with relief.

"Good evening," she said, slightly out of breath.

"Hello there. You're back, I see." Marcia was aware of Walter's eyes on her body, taking in her outfit.

"Yes," Marcia replied. "Sorry, am I disturbing you?"

Walter looked at her for a moment before responding. "No, I was just working on—something. How was the party? Your sister?"

"Confused, I think," Marcia said.

"About what?"

"Marriage, and a lot of things."

"That's too bad," Walter said, but his eyes caught hers and held them. Marcia felt her knees grow weak, and she fought to control the impulse to lean in and kiss him.

"I wanted to thank you for helping me today. I don't think I did that earlier."

"That's okay. My pleasure."

Pleasure. Marcia didn't know why, but as the word slipped off his tongue, she felt warmth between her thighs. She cleared her throat, gathering courage. "Do you want to come to my apartment for a minute?" she asked.

"Afraid of the dark?"

"And of things that appear in the night," she said with a smile.

"I understand." Walter stepped out into the hallway and shut his door before following her inside her apartment. Inside her apartment, Marcia suddenly became nervous when she realized they were alone. *Don't say something stupid.* It was hard to take her eyes off Walter. The blue sweats clung to his strong, lean frame and set off his hazel eyes. He hadn't shaved since that morning and the deep shadow on his face made him even sexier. Marcia took a deep breath.

"Please. Sit down," Marcia said as she tried to steady her nerves. "I'm just going to change."

As she walked toward the bedroom, Walter watched her. She looked tired, but she was still stunning. The way the black dress hung on her every curve quickened his pulse. Soft tendrils of her hair hung around her face, accentuating her finely-shaped jaw line. He could smell her delicate perfume, a wonderful floral scent, as she disappeared into the bedroom. Its fragrance beckoned to him and he swallowed to regain his composure.

"How was dinner?"

"It was fine. I mean, the food was anyway."

"What do you mean?"

"The conversation was kind of boring."

"Oh?"

"Yes," she called as she changed clothes, "Bankers. All they wanted to talk about was how much money they had and how much money they were going to make this year."

"I see," Walter said, smiling. "It was that kind of party."

"What kind?" Marcia called.

"The kind where the guests let other guests know exactly how rich they are. That kind."

Marcia laughed. "It was so pretentious. I'd have left earlier if it hadn't been Justin's party. I'd much rather spend my time doing more useful things."

"Like researching ghosts?"

Marcia laughed again. "Yes, like that. More interesting anyway."

"It speaks volumes that a dead woman is more interesting than a room full of bankers. But I have to say the more we research the life of this mysterious slave woman, the more intriguing she becomes," Walter said. He saw that the door was slightly ajar. *I wonder what she looks like…* He immediately wanted to kick himself for having that thought. *What are you, a Peeping Tom? Remember, she's a lady, and your friend.*

When Marcia came out in a T-shirt and sweats, her hair tied up in a ponytail, Walter again had to swallow to regain control of his emotions. Marcia Watkins was a very enticing woman, whether she was wearing an expensive evening gown or sweats. He liked the way the material clung to her curves. His eyes drifted the length of her and as she sat across from him on the sofa, he let himself imagine kissing her soft lips. Almost instantly, an image of Flo flashed before his eyes and he looked down, ashamed of the feelings he was having for another woman. He caressed the wedding band on his finger and fought to control the urge to kiss her.

Marcia propped her feet underneath her. "I hope you don't mind, but my feet hurt."

"No, of course not. You've had a long day."

"I have. It's like the time I tried to do the Louvre all in one day."

"In Paris?"

"Yes. Have you been?"

"Yes, I've been there, although I've actually been out of Louisiana only a few times. After I left the conservatory, my parents sent me on a three month trip to Europe. I liked Paris a lot. Then I went on my honeymoon to Mexico, and another time to Atlanta to see my friend Jasper who's got a home there. There's something about New Orleans. Gets in your blood, I guess. So, I tried to make a pianist out of myself, got married and found the job here, at the mansion. I've been here ever since."

"You never wanted to see America? Live in another state?"

"No, like I said, I'm just a New Orleans boy at heart. I've got everything I need right here. The apartment is my sanctuary. Most days, I stay here, except for when you're dragging me on ghost hunts," Walter laughed.

"I know. I'm sorry about that."

"No, it hasn't been so bad. I like a good mystery."

They fell silent for a moment.

"One thing to be said for New Orleans is that the food's great. It's spicy, not like in Vermont," Marcia said.

Walter shook his head. "Now Vermont, that's a place I couldn't live. Too cold for me. I like warm weather, always have, always will. Plus, I get a free apartment being landlord, and I've got the best renters there are. Never any trouble and barely ever here."

Marcia laughed. "Except for me. I've been bothering you since I got here!"

Walter gave her a warm smile. "You're not a bother. It's been a pleasure."

Walter's smile made Marcia tingly all over. She looked directly into his eyes. "Maybe you never had any incentive to leave New Orleans?"

Her look did not get the reaction she was hoping for. Walter shook his head. "I'm never leaving New Orleans. Flo's here. My place is with her."

"What if you meet someone else?"

"I don't believe that."

"Believe what?"

"I've always believed there was one special person for everyone. Flo was that special person for me."

"You plan to be alone for the rest of your life?"

"Yes. I couldn't do that to Flo. I can't betray her, I can't betray our love."

Marcia felt her heart sink. Walter Dufrane was an intriguing and sexy man, but he was also hopelessly in love with the memory of his wife.

"So what happens if you meet a woman you're interested in? You can't be alone forever."

"I'll never marry again. I mean that. I wouldn't be looking for anything serious even if I do meet someone I'm attracted to. It would never be about love. I'm not looking to love anyone."

So, he's not the one. She felt dejected. She wasn't interested in a fling, although the thought of making love to him had crossed her mind. She wanted someone to love who would love her back. *I guess we'll be friends. It's all for the best. I'm going back to Vermont by the end of next week and we'll probably never see each other again.* Suddenly, she didn't want to talk about love anymore. "I'm sorry, but maybe we can talk later? I'm beat."

"Long day. Ghost hunting will make anyone exhausted." Walter stood up.

"I suppose." She stood and yawned.

"Are you all right?"

"Just tired is all."

"You sure?" Before he could stop himself, Walter reached out and touched her cheek. Suddenly, he was staring right into her eyes and before she could react he had her face in his hands and was kissing her. His kiss was soft but demanding, and she opened her mouth to his kiss, overwhelmed by the warmth of his lips and their softness. She wrapped her arms around his neck and pressed her body against his. Then, just as the kiss began, it was over. Walter pulled away, his hands shaky.

"Oh my God, Marcia, I'm so sorry."

"Why?" She went toward him, but he backed away.

"I can't. I just can't."

"What? Kiss me?"

Walter nodded. "I shouldn't have done that. Will you forgive me?"

"Of course, but it's all right, Walter."

Walter shook his head. "No, it isn't. You're so sexy and beautiful and I would love to make love to you right here, right now—"

Marcia could feel her cheeks grow warm. She had never in her entire life been told she was sexy and she had never thought she was. But at that moment, as Walter's eyes roamed first her face and then her body, she did feel sexy, and she did feel desired. And for the first time, she felt like a woman.

"Walter…" She reached for him, but he moved away.

"And the thing is, we hardly know each other. But I like you. You're so smart and beautiful and I'm really attracted to you."

His words rang in her ears like music and she wanted to feel his arms around her, to kiss his soft lips and stare into his warm eyes. But as she made a move to approach him again, he turned away.

"Oh, I thought you were going to say that you didn't—"

"Let me finish."

"All right." Marcia said.

"I'm attracted to you, I'll admit that. And I can see that you're attracted to me. But if we made love, that's all I would want. I don't want to start something serious with you, not with anyone. I meant what I said earlier."

"Oh, I see." Marcia was crushed.

He turned back to face her. "I'm sorry. I don't want to hurt you. Listen, I'd better go."

Marcia was stunned. She wanted to grab Walter, to kiss him, to press her body against his and feel him inside her, but she stood there, not moving as he walked to the door. She wanted him, but she didn't want a fling.

Walter stood at the door for a moment, but then left without saying anything further. Marcia lay back down on the sofa. Before it had even begun, Walter Dufrane had taken himself out of a romance with her. She ran her hands the length of her body, wanting it to be Walter instead, caressing and kissing her. But she wouldn't be someone's one night stand.

~

She didn't know how long she had been asleep, but all at once, it started again—the cold chill in the room and the sense of *someone* in there besides her.

"Sam…"

Marcia sat up. The ghost was back. Marcia felt her heart pounding in her chest as she scanned the room, expecting to see the ghost woman. She wasn't as much afraid as she was anxious, waiting for the ghost to appear.

Then she saw the ghost of the slave woman standing near the bed, her stomach wound gaping. Marcia turned her face, suddenly feeling sick, but after a moment, she forced herself to look back. The ghost was now at the door and motioned for Marcia to follow. Marcia trembled with fear, but followed her to the door.

The slave woman was already in the hallway, which was wrapped in a thick fog of some kind. As she made her way down the hallway, Marcia noticed that everything from the paint on the doorways to the design of the hallway was different. There were portraits of people from another time hanging from the walls. She frowned. *Where did those come from?* She followed the ghost down the stairs and stopped cold when she saw that the portrait of Madame LaLaurie was hanging on the wall. The ghost was at the bottom of the steps, watching her. It was then that Marcia glanced down into the foyer and living room and saw that she had suddenly been transported back to another time. The living room was decorated with furniture from the 1800s and as she came down the staircase, the ghost disappeared. She looked frantically about and saw the ghost had opened the back door and gone into the garden. Outside, the ghost glanced down at a patch of roses in the back of the garden and then went back inside.

Marcia followed her slowly upstairs to the third floor. She had seen the staircase that led to the third floor, but the area had been blocked off with a special barrier. Now, as she made her way up the curved staircase, the stairs leading to the third floor attic were no longer roped off. Marcia turned to look back at the hallway, but it had disappeared in the fog. She slowly made her way up the creaky staircase, her hand on the cold railing. At the top of the staircase, she saw a room to the right, walked to it, and found a tastefully decorated dressing room and vanity with a gold-trimmed mirror. As she glanced behind her, she saw a chair and a beautiful gown with white lace laid out on it. When she walked forward to touch the dress, it disappeared.

Marcia turned and saw the ghost in the doorway. Gasping, she watched as the ghost vanished into an open door at the end of the hall. Taking a deep breath, she followed, her body quaking with fear. *The dead can't hurt you.*

The dead can't hurt you. Repeating that mantra over and over, she entered the room. At once she was overcome with the stench of rotting human flesh. Though she covered her mouth and nose with the sleeve of her pajama top, the odor was overwhelming. Then she saw the ghost woman gazing out a small window that looked out upon Royal Street. She indicated with her head the corner of the room and then she looked down at her stomach.

"I want Sam. Please...Sam..."

All at once, she disappeared. The stench dissipated after a moment and Marcia found herself alone in the room, the room where the woman must have been murdered. Why? Her owner's madness? Each time the slave woman had come to see her she had learned more of the slave's last days on earth. Why had she shown her the garden? Was there some connection between the slave girl who had jumped from the roof and the garden?

CHAPTER TEN

After a restless night, Marcia awoke groggy at midday to the sounds of a ringing telephone. It took her a moment to realize what the noise was before reaching over to the nightstand to pick up.

"Hello?"

"Hi, Marcia, it's me."

"Anna. Sorry, I was still asleep."

"Late night?"

"Sort of. I had a bad—nightmare."

"I'm sorry about that. But I'll pick you up for lunch and shopping in an hour. That'll make you feel better, won't it?"

Anna sounded happy and excited. Marcia wished she could stay in bed for the rest of the day, but she didn't want to disappoint her. "Okay."

"See you then."

An hour later, she had showered and changed and was on her way downstairs to the lobby to wait for Anna. As she shut her door, she suddenly felt a hand on her shoulder. She gasped, and hurriedly turned around.

Walter stood there. "I'm sorry, did I scare you?"

"Yes," Marcia said, catching her breath. She suddenly felt awkward and had trouble looking Walter in the eye. "I thought it was the—"

"Ghost? Sorry. I didn't mean to frighten you."

"It's all right," Marcia said nervously as she struggled to lock the door. She was embarrassed by what had happened the previous night and didn't want to deal with him at that moment. Besides that, she had been rejected in a way. Walter Dufrane wanted a one night stand and no matter how much she wanted him, she didn't want to be used like that. "I'm just on my way out to meet my sister."

"All right. I won't keep you. I just wanted to apologize for my behavior last night."

"You don't need to apologize, Walter. Let's just let it go. Now, I really must go."

Marcia made to move past him, but Walter grabbed her arm. His very touch sent flames of desire running through her body.

"Just hear me out. I wanted you last night."

"Shh…," Marcia said, looking around. "What if someone hears—"

"Who?" Walter said, lowering his voice and releasing her arm. "The slave woman? She won't care. Now listen to me. I wanted you last night. And I'm pretty sure by that kiss we shared that you wanted me, too. I hope I'm not mistaken in that."

"No," Marcia replied carefully, "You're not."

"Okay then. I don't want to hurt you."

"You've said that already."

"I meant it."

Marcia sighed. "It's okay, Walter. I appreciate your help yesterday, but maybe we should just avoid each other for the rest of the week. It's obvious you're not over your wife and I don't want to be someone's— fling. I'm looking for something that you're not ready to give. Anyway, I'm going back to Vermont in a week's time. I just don't see the point in continuing this…whatever this is."

"Friendship, I hope," Walter said. She saw a pained look on his face and her heart fell. Her body was screaming for his touch, his kiss, but her mind told her that now was the time to distance herself from Walter before she did something she would regret.

"Okay, friends. Now I have to go." Turning, she hurried down the hall to the stairs before he had a chance to reply and before she could change her mind and go back to him. *It's better this way. Now I can concentrate on helping with Anna's wedding and afterwards I'll go back to Vermont and my old life. I'll never have to think about him again.*

A LOVER'S LEGACY

After lunch, she and Anna went to a bridal boutique where Anna proceeded to try on every wedding dress they had. As her sister tried on her tenth dress, Marcia sat in the waiting room of the boutique, trying not to think about Walter. He could have made love to her last night, and she wouldn't have refused him. His honesty about not wanting to hurt her touched her. He did like her, of that she was certain. And he'd told her he found her beautiful. So why weren't they together? A part of her could understand his fear of not wanting to love someone again because he feared losing them. But the other part of her, the part that knew Walter wanted her as much as she did him, the part of her that felt they had a real connection, wanted to confront Walter about his reluctance to love again. *Maybe I should just forget about him.* But somehow, she couldn't.

Anna emerged, looking resplendent in a white, off-the-shoulder gown with an intricate lace pattern.

"Oh, Anna. You look beautiful."

Anna twirled in front of the mirror, her face full of excitement. "Just a few more days and I'll be married."

"Anna, have you decided what you want to do after you get married?"

"What do you mean?"

"I was serious about wanting you to pursue your dream. I think you should ask the manager to give you a chance. He has to. Look at the response you received the other night. You have such talent, Anna."

Anna wouldn't meet her eyes. She played nervously with the trim at the bottom of the dress. "I—I quit my job."

Marcia was stunned. "You quit?"

"Justin thought it was best."

"So you're unemployed?"

"As of last Friday," Anna said, smiling.

"I don't think that's anything to be proud of. What are you going to do, rely on Justin for money?"

"As a matter of fact, yes I am. Justin said he's going to take care of me, and that I don't have to worry about money ever again."

"That's generous of him. How do you feel about that?"

"I feel fine. I'm going to be his wife. There's nothing wrong with a husband supporting his wife. Besides, I hated waiting tables."

"It was a living."

Anna gave Marcia a look. "After I marry Justin, I'm going to be Mrs. Justin St. Jean, not some cocktail waitress at a two bit joint."

"At least you'll have plenty of time to pursue singing. Maybe you can—"

"Justin and I had a long talk yesterday. He was so angry with me and I hate it when he's angry. It's just not worth it to fight about this. He doesn't want me to sing professionally. I can always sing for fun. Singing can be a hobby—"

"Wait a minute. What do you mean, a hobby? Does Justin know how long you've wanted to be a professional singer? Does he know that you've dreamed of it all your life? Does he recognize your God-given talent?"

Anna turned away and pulled a black jewelry box from her purse. She walked back over to Marcia and opened the box. "Justin bought this for me. Do you like it?"

Marcia stared stone-faced at an exquisite sapphire and diamond necklace. "Very nice."

"What? You don't like it."

"You don't want to know what I don't like."

"What do you mean?"

"Every time you get into an argument, he buys you something. That's not going to work forever."

"He's sorry we fought."

"He's buying something, Anna, but it's not love."

"What is that supposed to mean?"

"I mean he's buying you."

Anna put the box back into her purse. "Justin was right."

"He was right about what?"

"Justin said that you're jealous, and that's why you're not happy I'm getting married. He thinks that you're trying to purposely destroy our happiness."

Jealous? Destroy? Anger boiled inside Marcia, ready to spill over, but she took a few breaths to try and calm herself down. "Justin St. Jean knows nothing about me. I'm not jealous that you're getting married. I admit, when I heard you were getting married, I pitied myself for still being alone. But I was happy for you. I still am. It's just I'm not sure Justin St. Jean has your best interests in mind."

"And you do?"

Marcia glared at Anna. "What's gotten into you, Anna?"

"Nothing, it's just that Justin thinks you influence me."

"I hope so. I'm your sister."

"Not in a good way."

"Oh?"

"Justin thinks—"

"Wait a minute," Marcia said, standing up. "I'm tired of hearing what Justin thinks. What do you think?"

Anna grabbed another dress off the rack and held it against her body in front of the mirror. "The other night was great, but I want to marry Justin and if that means sacrificing my dream to sing, then that's just what I'll have to do. I don't want to lose him."

"And you're afraid you will if you don't do what he wants?"

When Anna didn't answer her, Marcia knew the answer was yes. "So that was a farewell the other night at the Louis Armstrong?" Marcia asked.

"Yes," Anna said, turning to Marcia. "It was, and a kind one. I've finally had my chance at singing. I'm ready now to let go of that dream and settle down and start a family."

"Let go of that dream? What are you talking about? Anna, it's only the beginning. Please, don't let Justin take your dream away."

"He's not. We both decided—"

Marcia stood. "He decided."

"I'm getting married, Marcia. There's nothing you can say to dissuade me."

"So go ahead and get married. It's not the 1950s. Women can be married and have their own lives."

"Justin says that women in his family don't work. They've never worked."

"How nice for his family, but in our family women have *always* worked at something."

"Marcia, please. I've made up my mind. I think I'll try this one on next. Although the sleeves—"

Marcia crossed to Anna, standing behind her in the mirror's reflection. "What would Mom and Dad say about you giving up your dreams for a man? They wanted the best for you. They would be shocked you'd throw away a chance at a music career when it was so close to becoming a reality."

"What do you mean *close*? Ed felt pity for me. That's why he let me sing."

"But at least it was a chance and everyone in that room was captivated by you. Except for Justin."

"I know. He just thinks that sort of career isn't right for his future wife."

"I'm talking about you being up there singing. He didn't seem happy for you at all. He seemed angry."

"You're wrong. He was happy for me. It's just—"

"Stop making excuses for him, Anna."

"Marcia—"

Marcia shook her head. "Mom and Dad would be glad you found the man of your dreams, a man you love very much, but it would disappoint them for you to give up your dreams to marry him."

"Like I said before, Justin says I can continue singing, as a hobby. Now, I don't want to talk about it anymore. Here, try on this dress."

Marcia grabbed the dress Anna handed her and went into the dressing room. The dress was a perfect fit, but as she twirled in the mirror to view her back, the fit of the dress was the furthest thing from her mind.

"You look great! That dress doesn't need any adjustment at all."

"Thanks, but I don't want to just let this conversation drop."

"I don't want to talk about it anymore. I've already made up my mind. Nothing will change that. Now, turn around so I can see the back of the dress."

Marcia wanted to say more, but she lifted her arms and twirled in her off-the-shoulder, lavender Vera Wang gown. "Nice change of subject."

After Anna inspected Marcia's dress, she hugged Marcia. "Let's not be mad at each other, okay?"

"I'm not mad, Anna. I'm just—"

"I'm so happy you're here and you're going to be a part of the wedding. Don't worry so much, everything will work out," Anna said, cutting her off.

Marcia hugged Anna back. "All right. But I want you to do me a favor."

"What?" Anna looked worried.

"I just want you to come to me, about anything, okay? I'm here for you."

"All right."

Marcia returned to her room later that afternoon and walked quietly up the stairs. She could hear Walter playing the piano and wondered if he thought of his wife as he played. She leaned in and listened at the door as he played a piano concerto like an expert. She had wanted him last night, but she was glad she hadn't given in to her physical desire. If she and Walter had made love, she knew that at least for her, it would mean more than just sex. It was rare to meet someone who intrigued her, and Walter Dufrane was definitely intriguing. Yet he was so fixated on the past, Marcia didn't think that he would ever get over his wife. She wanted a future with someone who wanted a future with her. Standing there, listening to the melancholy music, she felt Walter's pain at the loss of his wife, but she still wanted to knock on the door and confront him. But she stopped herself. *Who are you to judge him?*

She went back to her room and spent the rest of the afternoon trying to read through the book she'd found in the library. As the light in her room grew faint, she changed out of her jeans and T-shirt and got into a nightgown. Switching on her bedside table lamp, she lay down on the bed. The French Quarter had gone through a lot of transitions and had changed hands from Spanish to French to Spanish to American. The book discussed slavery in the Quarter in only two paragraphs: one was regarding slave auctions and the other about the slaves' duties. There was no mention of mulattos or free people of color or what she had hoped, the quadroon balls. She shut the book and sighed. All during that time from the mid 1700s to the 1860s, slaves had worked in the Quarter as housemaids, cooks, footmen, coachmen, and personal atten-dants and had attended to the needs of wealthy Creoles and whites who lived in New Orleans. They had worked because they had to. If they didn't they were beaten, whipped or killed. A slave could be sold at any time, regardless of how they felt about it. They could be raped, and they could be maimed, and they could be killed, all at the whim of a master. *Is that what happened to the slave woman? Where did she live before she came to work for Madame LaLaurie? Where was she born?* Marcia shook her head and picked up the article regarding the slave who had been murdered in Pirate's Alley. She found herself reading and then rereading the article. The wording was curious. It didn't say that the slave was "murdered" but "found dead." *Hmmm…what would a slave be doing out alone in the middle of the night and how could his throat be slashed with-out it being murder?* Marcia glanced at the nightstand and saw that it was almost five o'clock. She desperately needed a nap and then dinner, which she planned to eat alone as Anna had to get back home to Justin.

Anna walked into the home in Vacherie to find Justin waiting for her in the sitting room.

"So you're home."

"Yes," Anna said, showing Justin her shopping bags. "Marcia and I were shopping all day. I finally found the dress and—"

"What did you and Marcia talk about?" Justin said, cutting her off.

"We talked about the wedding."

"And me, I presume?"

Anna set her bags down on the sofa and sat down. "What's all this about?"

"Have you told your sister that you no longer wish to pursue a singing career?"

"Yes. I did. Why are you checking up on me?"

"I just want to make it clear to her that you're going to be my wife and that she shouldn't interfere in our lives."

"She's my sister. She's always going to be a part of my life."

Justin sat down next to her. "But you'll be my wife in less than a week. I should be the most important person in your life."

"Why do you feel like you're in competition with my sister?"

Justin laughed. "Competition? Certainly not. I am simply making sure that you have your priorities in order. You are marrying me and making a life with me. If you wanted a life with your sister, you could move back to Vermont and the two of you could be old maids together."

Anna was taken aback. Justin had never spoken to her in such a manner before. "What's wrong with you, Justin? Why do you want to hurt my feelings?"

Justin immediately changed his demeanor. He gently took her hand and kissed it. "I'm sorry, my darling. It's just that I love you so much."

Anna stood. Suddenly she felt too exhausted to deal with Justin's demanding ways. "I'm going upstairs and have a bath. Call me when dinner is ready."

"Anna. Anna, come back here, please. Anna."

But Anna ignored him and went upstairs to her room.

Marcia hadn't realized she'd fallen asleep and awoke only when she heard the sounds of a police siren outside. She glanced at the clock on the nightstand and saw that it was twelve-thirty A.M. *Have I been asleep that long?* She took a look around the room and realized that she hadn't had such a good night's sleep in a long time. She felt her stomach rumbling and remembered that she hadn't had anything to eat since lunch. She looked around the apartment, but the only thing she found in the kitchen was a box of Wheat Thins. She opened the box and munched ravenously on the crackers.

I wonder if Walter is still awake. She thought about knocking on his door with the excuse of simply looking for a midnight snack. After all, it was late to go out for food, especially when she didn't know where to go. Suddenly she didn't feel like eating anymore, but she really wanted to see Walter and apologize for her behavior in the hallway. She put down the box of Wheat Thins and grabbing her robe, threw it on over her nightgown and opened the door. The hallway was empty, so she shut the door quietly. As she approached Walter's door, she could feel her heart pounding. She took a deep breath, trying to calm down. After lightly tapping on the door, she heard footsteps.

Walter flung open the door and stood there dressed only in a pair of blue pajama bottoms. Marcia swallowed, trying not to stare at his muscular chest and arms.

"Hello. You're still up?" she said, aware her voice was slightly shaking.

"Yes," Walter said, running his hand through his hair. "I couldn't sleep."

"Oh," Marcia said, feeling uncomfortable. "I took a chance you'd be up. I…"

"Would you like to come in?"

Marcia was taken aback by the question. "Sure, just for a minute."

Walter slowly opened the door wider for her and she stepped inside a stylishly designed living room with a grand piano in one corner. Marcia glanced to her right and saw a designer's kitchen, complete with Viking stove and All Clad cookware. Two large shelves contained numerous books. On the walls hung tasteful photographs of New Orleans and the living room was decorated in desert colors, soft reds and browns, suggesting a woman's touch.

"This is a beautiful apartment, Walter."

"Thank you. I should have invited you in earlier, it's just…"

"I understand."

"Please, sit down."

Marcia took a seat on one of the sofas. Strewn across the coffee table was sheet music.

"Are you working on a piece of music?"

But Walter did not answer her. He'd been thinking about her all night, unable to concentrate on anything else. He'd been trying to sum up the courage to knock on her door and apologize when she knocked on his door. Walter watched her, the way she moved, the way the light played up her delicate features, the womanly shape of her and was unable to stop the uncontrollable desire he had for her.

"Listen, Walter, I'm sure you're tired—"

Before she could say anything further, Walter grabbed her and pressed his lips against hers. Marcia was taken aback by the urgency of his kiss and before she could stop herself, she was responding, her lips seeking the same pleasure his did. Walter pressed his body up against her and his tongue sought hers. Suddenly, he pulled away.

"Do you want me to stop?" he asked breathless.

"No," she moaned, pulling him back toward her. She responded, opening her mouth to his searching tongue. Her hands roamed his chest and shoulders and at that instant, she wanted him inside her. She moaned with pleasure as Walter trailed kisses all across her face to her throat.

"Please…" she moaned. "Please don't stop."

Walter's hands roamed her body, one pushing aside the robe while the other sought the silky softness of her breasts. He expertly rubbed the tip of her right nipple, while the other hand sought the wet folds of her femininity. He opened her and gently rubbed the pulsating nub, while he moved his head down and began to lick her erect nipple.

"I want you…"

"Yes," she moaned, and before she could react, Walter lifted her and carried her to his bedroom and laid her down on the bed. He began to undress her, his hands caressing her body as he removed her robe and then unbuttoned the nightgown. He then slid out of his pajama bottoms and got into bed with her and continued kissing her, his passion frenzied. Marcia was overwhelmed by his desire for her and as he gently slipped off her panties and parted her with his tongue, she cried out with pleasure.

"Oh, Walter, yes!"

He was inside her, and she opened to him, her rhythm matching his as their passion grew even more frenzied.

"You're so beautiful. Oh, Marcia it's wonderful," Walter whispered in her ear and she clung to him as she cried out in ecstasy.

CHAPTER ELEVEN

When Marcia awoke, she was lying in Walter's arms. He was still asleep, his mouth slightly open. She smiled, recalling his cries of pleasure, and gently caressed his face. Then, just at that instant, the mood was broken, replaced by an overwhelming sense of guilt. *How is Walter going to act? Why did I make love to him? Is that all he wanted from me?*

Walter stirred and Marcia pulled the sheet up to cover her nakedness. He opened his eyes and seeing her, smiled sleepily. "Good morning…"

"Morning," she replied nervously. She wanted to get out of his bed and apartment as fast as she could. *What have I done?*

"You look beautiful," he said, as he tried to pull her back down to him. But Marcia edged away.

"I have to get going," she said, trying to wrap the sheet around her.

Walter slowly sat up. "What's wrong?"

"I—I don't know."

"Of course you do."

"We shouldn't have—made love."

"Are you sorry we did? I'm not."

Marcia looked at him in surprise. "You're not?"

"No. It was one of the most fantastic nights of my life and I have to thank you."

That's all he wanted. Sex. I'm a fool. Marcia forgot the sheet and got out of bed, hurriedly searching for her clothes on the floor.

"Marcia, what are you doing?"

"Getting out of here."

"Why? What's wrong?"

"You got what you wanted last night. There's no need to say anything more."

Walter wrapped the sheet around his waist and slowly got out of bed. "We both got what we wanted last night."

Marcia glared at him. "What's that supposed to mean?"

"You came to me—"

Marcia felt tears come to her eyes. "Oh great. I'm some desperate old maid, throwing myself on you. Thanks. Thanks a lot."

She grabbed her nightgown and tried to put it on. She didn't care about the robe; she just had to get out of there.

"Marcia. Slow down. Hear me out."

"No. You've told me before that all you want is sex and now that you've got it…" Tears rolled down her cheeks.

Walter grabbed her and pulled her to him. "Oh, Marcia, no, please stop crying, please."

Marcia wept against his chest.

Walter held her head in his hands and made her look at him. "I know what I said, but I was a fool. Marcia, I can't stop thinking about you. You're the first woman since Florence who's made me feel like a man. Marcia, I…"

"What?" she said, staring up at him.

"It's crazy, but I love being with you. You've gotten under my skin."

She smiled at him through her tears. "Have I?"

"You're wonderful, Marcia. Hasn't anybody ever told you that?"

She shook her head.

"Those Yankees up there in Vermont really are blind."

Marcia laughed as Walter wiped away her tears with his fingertips and gently kissed her.

"There, better?"

She nodded and rested her head against his chest.

"But what about what you said?"

"About not wanting to start something serious?"

"Yes."

"I don't feel that way anymore. But I want to go slowly. Okay?"

"All right," Marcia said, happy to be in his arms.

"Now, how about some breakfast?"

"Sounds great. I'm starved."

"Breakfast will be ready in a jiffy. Why don't you shower if you want while I—"

"No, I'll help. Lead the way."

Twenty minutes later, they were in the kitchen, working side by side. Walter watched as Marcia, dressed in one of his T-shirts and a pair of his boxer shorts, expertly whipped up blueberry crepes with fresh cream. There hadn't been a woman in that kitchen since Flo, but somehow Marcia being there just seemed right. She'd grabbed a cookbook off the shelf for the blueberry crepe recipe and it hadn't bothered him. He set the table, watching her, and he liked the wonderful feeling of having her there with him. Walking back into the kitchen, he came up behind her, gently kissing her neck.

"You're a natural cook. I may just have to ask you to move in."

"All right," Marcia said, laughing. "I'll just move my business down here."

"I'm sure you'd have no trouble finding clients."

"Be serious."

"I am," he said, turning her to face him. "After all, you like New Orleans, don't you?"

"Of course I do."

"And we haven't solved the mystery of the ghost yet, so you may just have to stay."

Marcia laughed and gently pushed him away. "Let me cook. We'll talk about the ghost after these crepes are done or else they'll burn."

A few minutes later, they sat at the dining table, eating blueberry crepes with coffee. As Walter ate, he savored each delicious bite. He hadn't felt so good in a long time and it wasn't the fact that he'd made love to a beautiful woman. It was the particular woman who made him happy. Her very presence lifted his spirit. He reached for her hand. "Marcia?"

"Yes?"

"Thank you for last night."

Marcia felt her cheeks grow warm, but smiled. "Thank you."

"I meant what I said. I—can't stop thinking about you. I—don't want you to leave."

Marcia looked at him in surprise. "Walter—"

"You're the best thing that's happened to me since—since—"

"Flo?" Marcia said quietly.

"Yes." Walter stood and brought her picture back to the table. "This is Flo."

Marcia took the picture from him and stared at the photograph of the woman with dark eyes and beautiful dark skin. "She was beautiful."

"Yes."

"And so young." She smiled at Walter and handed the picture back to him. "Thank you for sharing her picture with me. She must have been a wonderful woman."

"She was," Walter said. Suddenly a thought occurred to him. "What are you doing today?"

"I don't have plans. Anna hasn't—"

"I want to show you something. Can I?"

"Of course."

~

After showering and dressing, Walter and Marcia walked down Royal Street and turned onto North Rampart. They walked up toward 759 North Rampart Street.

"I haven't been by here in two years. Not since…"

Walter held his breath, but was shocked when he saw that the sign for Flo's Joint still hung in the building's window. He couldn't believe that the owner hadn't leased the place yet.

"I can't believe it's still here."

"This is Flo's Joint?"

They both peered through the dirty windows and saw the empty space, devoid of light and furniture. Plywood leaned against one wall, alongside paint canisters. "I can't believe it. It's just as I left it. Unfinished."

"It's amazing. How come no one's rented this place yet?"

"That's what I'm going to find out." Walter buzzed the landlord, who let them into the building. Stu, the landlord, explained that because of the economy no one had been able to afford the place. In fact, along North Rampart Street, many of the old clubs lay empty. Stu left them alone to take a look at the space and as Walter wandered around, looking at the unfinished room, Marcia suddenly had an idea.

"Walter."

"Yes?"

"Why don't you open this place up?"

Walter looked at her in shock. "Open it up?"

"Right. I don't think it's coincidence that we came by and this place wasn't rented. It's just as you left it. Wouldn't it be a wonderful legacy and tribute to open this place for Flo? In her memory?"

Walter thought about it for a moment. "No, this place...it killed her."

"No, Walter, it didn't. You didn't either. Cancer did. It's not your fault. Stop blaming yourself. I never met Flo, but I don't think she'd want you torturing yourself like this."

Walter considered Marcia's words for a moment. All at once he knew she was right. Flo would have been furious at him for locking himself away for the past two years and letting life pass him by.

"You're right. You're so right."

Marcia walked toward him and took his arm. "Imagine, imagine this place with people dancing, eating, listening to live jazz...living life. That's what Flo would want, I think."

Walter turned to her, tears in his eyes. "Oh, Marcia, you're right. You're so right." She held him to her and suddenly another idea occurred to her. "And I have just the person to liven up the joint with her voice."

"Who?"

"My sister Anna."

"Your sister?"

"Of course she'll audition for you. But with her voice and you on the piano, this place will be packed."

"All right," Walter said, nodding, getting excited by the idea himself. "All right."

"How long do you think before you can open up?"

"I don't know. Maybe a few weeks," he said as he took another look around the space. "Most of the heavy work is done. All I need to do is get the carpenters and painters and…"

As he talked, Marcia smiled to herself. Now all she had to do was convince Anna to audition. As she glanced toward the narrow stairway that led to the attic upstairs, she immediately recalled what she'd seen the other night.

"I didn't tell you what happened the other night."

Walter turned to her. "What?"

"I can't believe I forgot until now. I must have thought it was a bad dream. Maybe it was, but—"

"What? What happened?"

"I saw the ghost again. I think she—she showed me what happened."

"To her? You mean to her?"

"Yes," Marcia said. "I think so anyway. It was so horrible. She led me to the staircase upstairs and I saw it all."

"The staircase that's blocked off?"

"Yes."

"But I've got the key—"

"I know, but it wasn't blocked off. It was like I was taken back in time, to her time and it was happening right then. She showed me the room where she died and I could feel her pain and smell decaying flesh. Oh Walter," she turned to him, "you do believe me don't you?"

"Of course I do."

"Why me? I keep asking myself that."

"Do you know why?"

She looked him in the eyes and knew the answer. "Maybe because I listened."

"Maybe. I don't know, Marcia. It's all so strange."

"But you'll still help me."

"Of course. That's what I was going to tell you. I remembered a place that keeps old historical documents. The St. James Historical Society Museum just might be the answer."

"Really?"

"Let me talk to Stu and see about renting this place and then we'll head over there and see if we can't help this ghost find 'Sam.'"

Marcia hugged Walter. "Thank you."

"Thank *you*, Marcia."

Marcia called Anna to let her know that she and Walter were going over to the St. James Historical Society Museum, but the maid told her that Anna and Justin were out getting Anna's wedding gown altered. She left a message to have Anna call her when she got back.

On the drive over to the St. James Historical Society Museum they were both quiet, lost in thought. Marcia's thoughts were all in a jumble. She was falling in love with Walter but he lived in New Orleans and she in Vermont. *Is he serious about me moving in with him?* No, she knew he liked her and wanted to get to know her better, but he also wanted to take it slow. He'd said it so she'd know how much he liked her. But how could their relationship work out? Could she move her business down to New Orleans? She loved the

city and the idea of being close to Anna appealed to her. She hadn't
been able to convince Anna to postpone the wedding and felt quite
certain that in less than a week, Anna would be Mrs. Justin St. Jean,
for better or for worse. But if she could get Anna to audition for
Walter, maybe she could have both Justin and her dream of singing.
Marcia picked up Walter's hand and held it in her own. She wouldn't think about all that now.

An hour later, they exited off River Road and walked into the
museum. They found the director's office in the back with a sign on
the door that read RICHARD PEAKING, DIRECTOR.

They knocked on the door.

"Come in," called a deep, friendly voice.

They entered a cramped office with a window that faced a
garden at the back of the building. An elderly man with white hair
sat behind the desk, his thick glasses perched precariously at the end
of his nose. He stood and smiled when he saw Marcia and Walter.

"Good afternoon. How are you folks today?"

"Fine," Walter said. "I'm Walter Dufrane, and this is Ms.
Marcia Watkins."

The man shook their hands warmly. "Richard Peaking. Please,
sit down there."

They sat down.

"What can I do for you folks?"

Walter looked at Marcia. "Do you want me—?"

"Sure, go on," Marcia replied.

"Mr. Peaking—" Walter began.

"Call me Richard. Mr. Peaking was my father."

Walter smiled. "All right, Richard, we need some information."

"What kind of information?"

Walter looked over at Marcia again. Should they tell this man
they needed information on a ghost and risk his thinking they were
crazy? Marcia cleared her throat and continued.

"You see, I'm staying at LaLaurie Mansion and am interested in finding out as much as I can about the slaves that lived and worked there."

Richard smiled. "Nice place. But you're not here to learn about slave history. You're on a ghost hunt, aren't you?"

Marcia looked at Walter. "Why do you say that?"

"I've been in this business too long not to spot a couple of ghost hunters. You're not interested in what slaves did on a plantation and how they lived. You want to know how and why the LaLaurie slaves died."

Marcia nodded. "You've caught us. Yes, we do."

"Why?"

Walter cleared his throat. "Just curiosity."

"Not good enough."

"All right, Richard. I'll tell you the truth. I saw—something."

"Something? What?"

"A ghost," Marcia said tentatively.

"A real live one? No pun intended, of course."

"Yes. I've actually seen it several times."

Richard sat back, nodding his head. "This isn't a joke?"

Walter answered for her. "No. I've never seen anything, but I've heard things now and again and I've been living there for years. But I believe Marcia saw something."

Richard looked at Marcia. "I believe in ghosts. We sure do have our share in New Orleans." He leaned forward. "What exactly did you see?"

"I saw a slave woman who was horribly wounded. She asked me to help her find 'Sam.'"

"Sam? Maybe her husband or kid?"

"We don't know," Walter said.

"Maybe another slave?" Marcia offered.

"Do you know how many slaves were named Sam or Tessa? Thousands."

"We just want to find one Sam."

"So what kind of information do you need?"

"Maybe documents showing bills of sale, something that would help identify her. Surely there are records somewhere," Marcia said.

"Most of the LaLauries' records burned in that fire, if they ever really existed. Madame LaLaurie didn't follow the letter of the law acquiring her slaves and when they disappeared, she got new ones, without ever explaining what happened to the old ones. Many of the slave sales were 'under the table,' troublesome slaves that slave owners wanted to get rid of. Sometimes slaves were traded for other property, maybe a fine antique. I mention this because Madame LaLaurie was quite an antique collector."

"Troublesome slaves?" Marcia asked.

"Sure, maybe slaves who refused to work or got too old, or," Richard shifted in his chair, "indiscretions the slave master didn't want anyone to know about."

"Indiscretions?"

"The institution of slavery was not one of the South's greatest moments. It was not uncommon for masters and slaves to have relations. The result being—"

"Mixed children. Mulattoes."

"Right you are. Back then, they referred to them as quadroons, or free people of color."

"The slave I saw was light-skinned. Do you think maybe she was the result of a rape or a relationship between an owner and a slave?"

"It's possible," Richard said.

"Do you have any idea where an account of the slaves who worked at LaLaurie might be?" Walter asked.

"The attic's full of old papers and letters from that time. They're not in any sort of order. But if you want, I'll let you take a look. Maybe, just maybe, there might be something in those records about the LaLaurie slaves."

Marcia could hardly contain her excitement. "Can we have a look, please? We won't stay long."

"Right. Let me get my keys."

Marcia beamed at Walter as Richard got his keys and they followed him up the stairs to the attic. They walked into a dusty, cramped room which was wall to wall file cabinets and boxes.

"Here we are. The files aren't in any specific order, but help yourself. I'll be back in an hour to see how you're getting on."

"Thanks, Richard. We'll try not to make too much of a mess," Walter said, looking around in bewilderment.

Richard smiled. "Too late. I'm gonna go back into my office and see if there's not something in the files there about the slave auction after the fire."

"Thanks, Richard. We appreciate any help you can give."

"Sure, no problem. See you in a while."

He departed, leaving Walter and Marcia in the cramped airless attic room. Walter sighed and looked over at Marcia. "Ready when you are."

"Let's get cracking."

———

"No, no Sam."

It was an hour later and they had yet to find anything in the files or the boxes so far. Marcia threw her hands up in frustration, then sank back onto the floor. "What's the point? We're never going to find anything in this mess. Let's give up. It was a stupid idea anyway. What was I thinking? That I could help a ghost?"

"Don't talk like that. We're close. I can feel it."

"The only thing I feel is hunger. It doesn't matter. Let's just go."

Walter dropped the bunch of folders in his hand and sank down next to Marcia. "Later I'll buy you the biggest steak dinner you've ever had, but for now, we've got work to do. Come on." He stood and held out his hand, which she took. As she stood, Walter pulled her toward him and kissed her.

"I like that," she said, wrapping her arms around him.

"So do I, but dessert later. Come on, we've got a bunch of files to go through and not much time left."

She was tired, but went back to work. Looking around the room, she saw a box resting on top of one of the file cabinets in the back. Reaching up, she pulled it down, surprised by its weight. As she sorted through the box, she sighed again in frustration. It held old letters, most of them in French.

"Most of these are in French. How am I supposed to know what they say?"

"I can read a little French. I'll look through the letters that are in French after I've finished with these boxes."

"You know French?"

"*Oui, Madame, un petit peu.*"

Marcia laughed. "I'm impressed."

"That's good, I like to impress you," Walter said, smiling at her from across the room.

Marcia set the files in French to one side and was about to put the lid back on the box when something at the bottom caught her eye. She pulled the tattered piece of paper from the box and stared at it, not believing what she was seeing.

"Walter."

"Hmm?"

"I think I've found it."

"What?"

"I've found it! I've found it!"

Walter dropped the box he was looking through and hurried over to her. "What?"

"Look!"

Marcia held a clipped copy of an old *New Orleans Bee* in her hand. At the top was a headline that read: MAY 5TH, 1834. NOTICE OF LALAURIE SLAVE AUCTION.

Walter hugged Marcia to him. "I knew you'd find it!"

"What's it say? It's so hard to read."

"Be careful now. Don't rip it."

Walter placed the clipping on top of another box and spreading it carefully, began to read:

MAY 5, 1834: NOTICE OF LALAURIE SLAVE AUCTION
Eight negroes will be offered for sale at 12:00 P.M., being the entire stock of Dr. LaLaurie of Royal Street. The Negroes are in good condition, some of them very prime and good house servants. Also being offered one mulatto girl of rare personal quality. Any gentleman or lady wishing to purchase can come to Crawford's Auction House, Canal Street on such time and date.

Herewith are the Negroes for sale:
Deekin, Negro, forty and two, driver
Ethan, Negro, forty, coachmen
Ernest, Negro, twenty and two, butler
Philip: Negro, thirty and four, gardener
Meg, Negress, thirty and five, cook
Tilly, Negress, eighteen, cook and housemaid
Margery, Negress, twenty and one, housemaid
Aimee, mulatto, sixteen, housemaid

"It can't be her," Marcia said disappointed. "This is almost a month after the fire."

"You're right. And there's no mention of a Sam."

Marcia looked over the article and a thought suddenly occurred to her. "Maybe she was related to one of the women. Maybe one of them was her mother."

"It's a long shot. How will we ever know?"

"See if we can find out where the women were sold."

"Okay."

They began to search through the box, hoping it would yield clues to the slave woman's identity.

"Here!" Walter pulled out a bill of sale. "It's dated May 5, 1834. It says 'Meg, Philip and Aimee being sold on this day to Mr. Matthew Abernathy for use at his residence at 2642 River Road, Vacherie.'"

Marcia looked up, startled. "What was that address again?"

"2642 River Road."

"Justin's home in Vacherie has that same address."

"Justin's ancestors must have bought the place from this Mr. Abernathy."

That name's familiar. Suddenly, Marcia knew where she'd heard it before. "There's a portrait of Mr. Abernathy in the hallway of Justin's home. I think Evers, the butler, said that they were related in some way to the St. Jeans. Maybe through marriage."

Walter flipped the article over and found a letter attached. "There's more, a letter. Meg, Negress and Aimee, mulatto, being mother and child, are to be returned to the residence from where they were originally purchased. Mr. Abernathy requests credit of payment for loss of slave, Desiree, mulatto, 18.

"Is the slave woman Desiree? Meg and Aimee were born on the Abernathy plantation. Are they related? There has to be a connection."

"That's why Abernathy wants repayment. Desiree was his slave," Marcia said.

"But what was she doing at LaLaurie Mansion and how long was she there?"

Richard knocked on the door. "Did you find anything?"

"Yes, this," Walter said, walking over with the article in his hand. Richard took it and read it over. "Would you look at that."

"We need to know what happened to Desiree. She might be our ghost."

"Hmmm. Tell you what I'll do. There's got to be some information in the museum archives, but I can't look through them until after the museum is closed. I'll look tonight and see if I can dig up anything else about the LaLaurie slaves."

"That would be great. Thanks for your help," Marcia said as she stretched her arms. Exhausted, she was looking forward to a rest. Her head was spinning from the airless, cramped room.

"Here's the number at the mansion," Walter said as he handed Richard a card.

"Thanks. I'll give you a call if I find something, all right?"

"Terrific. Come on, Marcia."

Richard walked them to the door and they waved good-bye as they made their way to Walter's car.

CHAPTER TWELVE

It was late afternoon by the time Walter and Marcia got back to the mansion.

"You're having dinner with your sister tonight?"

"Yes."

"Oh."

"Why don't you join us?"

"Really?" Walter seemed surprised.

"Sure. Anna won't mind, and I don't care if Justin does."

Walter laughed and grabbing her, pulled her to him. "Till later?"

"See you around eight," she whispered and kissed him before walking into her own apartment. She immediately saw a note underneath her door.

Hi. Stopped by, but you weren't here. Justin says hi. He has a meeting tonight and can't join us for dinner. But call me when you get back in and we'll have dinner together. I hope you had a nice day.

Love, Anna

Marcia somehow doubted that Justin had sent his regards to her. It was obvious by his demeanor toward her at his party that he didn't like her, nor did he trust her with Anna. She didn't care. She didn't trust Justin St. Jean and she was going to find a way to prove to Anna that he wasn't right for her.

Marcia walked over to the phone and picked it up. Before she dialed Anna's number, something stopped her. Suddenly she had an idea, a sure fire way of knowing just what kind of man Justin St. Jean was. She dialed the operator.

"Hello? Operator? Do you have a listing for a Beatrice Beauregard? Hmm? That's right. And what address are you showing? Great. Thank you."

Marcia wrote down the address and hung up.

~

Marcia took the St. Charles streetcar and got off at 3630 St. Charles Avenue. She checked the address and looked up at another magnificent mansion in the Greek revival style. Walking to the front door, she rang the bell. When she didn't get a response, she rang it again. Finally, she heard footsteps coming toward the door and a moment later, a pretty girl in her early twenties hesitantly opened the door. She had a glass in her hand which was filled with what smelled and looked like gin. She swayed slightly at the door.

"Miss Beatrice Beauregard?"

"Yes? Who wants to know?"

"I'm Marcia Watkins. I—this is awkward. May I come in and speak with you for a moment?"

After a moment, the woman slowly opened the door and motioned her in. Marcia wiped her feet before stepping into the exquisitely decorated home. To the left was an elegant parlor that looked out onto a patio and well-designed garden. Clearly, money had not been the motivation behind Beatrice's marriage to Justin.

"Come on in," Beatrice said as she walked unsteadily into the parlor and sat down on a brown leather armchair. As she chugged back her drink, Marcia took a seat on the sofa across from her.

"Sorry if I was rude. It's just that we get a lot of tourists who want to photograph this house and sometimes it gets kind of irritating."

"That's no problem. However, I'd like to talk to you about a personal matter."

"Go ahead. Want something to drink?" Before Marcia could answer, she was already at the bar, pouring some tonic water into glasses. Marcia noticed that Beatrice kept spilling the liquid as she tried to hold the bottle steady over the glasses. *She's really drunk.* Beatrice added a little bit of gin to Marcia's glass, but filled her own to the rim with gin. Walking back over, she handed Marcia her glass, and sat back down. Marcia took a sip and almost choked. Beatrice had added more gin than Marcia had realized. She set the glass down on the table.

"So, what do you want to talk about?"

"Were you married to Justin St. Jean?"

"Why do you ask?"

"My sister Anna is engaged to Justin and I was wondering if you could tell me…"

Beatrice laughed. "So Justin's getting married again?"

"Yes, next Saturday."

"I knew he would. A man like him needs a woman in his life."

"What do you mean?"

"I assume you've met him?"

"Yes, I have."

"Justin is extremely possessive, a control freak. He's also insanely jealous."

The gut feeling that Marcia had about Justin was coming to life. It wasn't just Anna he liked to control.

"How long were you married?"

"Just a year."

"Can I ask you why you married him?"

"That's a funny question."

"I only meant—"

"Go on. Say it."

"You're already wealthy, or at least your parents are."

Beatrice shrugged. "It's going to sound corny, but I thought I loved him. He was a real charmer, at first, and I felt sorry for him because he'd just lost his wife."

"Tiffany."

"Right. Tiffany. That was her name."

Marcia picked up her glass and took a tiny sip. "Did you know her?"

"Of her. She and Justin were married for quite a few years before she died. When I met Justin I was trying to get out from under my parents' control. I was looking for freedom." She shook her head and took another sip of gin. "I was just a stupid kid."

"How long did you and Justin date?"

"A couple of months. He asked me right away. My parents were all for it. He came from a good family, was rich and educated. I was young and kind of wild. They thought he'd settle me down."

"Were you happy with him?"

"At first. But when we got back from the honeymoon, he became completely possessive. He wouldn't let me go out without him and he was always checking up on me like he didn't trust me. It was a bad time for me. He was so—suffocating. I couldn't even breathe without him being there. And his mother—" Beatrice rolled her eyes.

"What about her?" Marcia asked.

"Mrs. St. Jean was so controlling. Bossing everyone around, most of all me. Justin started to change. He didn't want me out of his sight. I guess she was telling him that I was young and needed to be supervised. It got old. He'd even get mad if I wanted to visit my parents! I felt like I was in prison. I was young, I wanted to be in New Orleans where things happened, but he said that it was time to settle down and start thinking about starting a family. You know, real old-fashioned stuff."

"Oh? And did you?"

"We tried to start a family, we really did, but I couldn't get pregnant. So I went to the doctor." She took another sip of her drink. "Doctor told me I couldn't have kids."

"I'm sorry to hear that."

Beatrice shrugged. "I never really wanted kids anyway. I knew Justin did so I wanted to get pregnant to please him. Never wanted to raise them, though. Justin said we'd get the kid a nanny so I wouldn't have to be bothered, which suited me just fine. I like to travel and shop and you can't do that with a dribbling kid at your side."

"Was there a reason?"

"For what?"

"Your not being able to conceive?"

"I guess I'm just not able. Something wrong with my cervix. I'd had a couple of miscarriages before I met Justin."

"Did Justin know that?"

"Nope, never told him."

Marcia wondered if Justin St. Jean would have married a woman who was unable to bear his children. Highly doubtful. Not to mention the fact that he didn't know about her earlier pregnancies. Somehow she didn't think Beatrice's family money would have been enough.

"How did Justin react to your not being able to bear children?"

Beatrice looked at her as if she were crazy. "He divorced me."

Marcia was alarmed. "What? That's why you got divorced?"

Beatrice nodded, slightly slurring her words. "The uh—what do you call it—prenup—said that if I was 'barren' Justin had the right to divorce me. Apparently Tiffany couldn't have kids and Justin didn't want to risk remaining married to a woman who couldn't have kids."

"Justin really wanted kids?"

"He wants an heir."

"And you had a prenup?"

"Yeah, a prenuptial agreement."

"I'm not aware of a prenup involving my sister. She's never mentioned one."

"There's one all right. Justin never marries without one. Even he and Tiffany had one. Just ask your sister." She smiled at Marcia. "Go ahead. I bet you she knows all about the prenup. Justin certainly didn't waste time showing it to me."

"I will." *Prenuptial agreement? Why didn't Anna tell me about that?*

"Let me give you some advice for your sister."

"Okay."

"Tell her Justin St. Jean, that marrying Justin St. Jean, was the biggest mistake of my life. He's a man who is used to getting what he wants. She needs to be sure she's ready to be married, especially to him. I wasn't."

Marcia stood. She had to see Anna and warn her. "Thanks for talking to me."

"Sure, no problem. See yourself out?"

"All right."

As Marcia turned to walk to the door, she saw Beatrice walk to the bar and pour herself another drink. She felt sorry for the young woman, but at that moment the only thing on her mind was talking to Anna and finding out the truth about Justin.

CHAPTER THIRTEEN

Marcia took a cab back to the mansion and called Anna, asking her to come over as soon as possible. While she waited for Anna to arrive, she nervously paced the room. *If you hurt my sister, Justin St. Jean, just watch out.*

Finally, she heard a knock at the door and hurried to open it. Anna stood there, dressed casually in black slacks and a tan blouse.

"Here I am!" Anna beamed. "Ready for dinner?"

"Uh, I want to talk to you, Anna," Marcia said. "Sit down."

Anna looked worried. "Is everything all right?"

"Yes, well, no, it isn't," Marcia said as she sat down next to her on the sofa. "I've just been to see Beatrice."

"Beatrice? Justin's ex? Why?" Anna asked, puzzled.

"I had to talk to her and find out all I could about Justin St. Jean." Marcia looked at Anna. "I don't trust him and I don't want you to marry him."

"What?" Anna stood up.

"Sit down, Anna, and hear me out."

Anna slowly sat back down. "What's happened?"

"Just hear me out, okay?"

"Fine. But why were you checking up on him?" Anna asked.

"I wanted to meet Beatrice to find out why she and Justin didn't work out. She told me that Justin made her sign a prenuptial agreement."

She paused and looked at Anna for a reaction. Anna shrugged. "So?"

"She said Justin wouldn't get married without one."

"But he and I don't have one."

"Are you sure?"

"Positive. He hasn't even mentioned a prenup to me."

"Don't be too sure he won't. But it gets worse."

"What?"

"Beatrice told me that Justin was possessive, controlling, and would barely let her out of the house."

"He's a little possessive, but—"

"Hear me out."

"Okay."

"It gets worse. When Beatrice found out she couldn't have kids, Justin divorced her."

Anna sat back, shocked. "What?"

"It's true. It was in the prenuptial agreement."

Anna shook her head. "I don't believe it."

"Believe it. Beatrice said that Justin had a prenup with Tiffany, too."

"Oh my God! What should I do?"

"I think you should confront him. He says he loves you, but what will he do if you can't have children?"

"The doctor said I'm fine—"

"You never know. You have to do this, Anna. Go home and talk to him. Please. Marrying him could be the biggest mistake of your life. Beatrice told me it was the biggest mistake of hers."

"I'll go home now. Justin hasn't left for his meeting yet. Oh, Marcia, what if—"

Marcia hugged Anna. "Don't worry. Things will be okay. Do you want me to go with you?"

Anna hesitated. "No. I have to do this alone."

"Call me as soon as you know what's going on."

"Okay," Anna said.

They embraced again and Anna left.

After Anna left, Marcia lay down on her bed and waited anxiously for Anna's call. Even if Justin hadn't shown it to Anna, she knew he had drawn up a prenuptial agreement for her sister to sign. Of that, she was certain. *Oh Anna…I never wanted to see you hurt.*

It was obvious that she couldn't go back to Vermont, at least not for a while. She needed to be here for her sister. There was a knock at the door and she got up to answer it.

"Yes?"

"It's me. Walter. I've—"

She opened the door and as soon as she saw him, she started to cry. Walter looked at her in surprise and walked her over to the sofa.

"What's wrong?"

"I just found out that Justin had Beatrice sign a prenuptial agreement."

"Beatrice? Justin's ex-wife? You went to see her?"

"I had to know firsthand what kind of man he is. Beatrice said she was miserable. Justin was controlling, possessive, and worse of all, he divorced Beatrice when she couldn't have children. Anna thinks Justin really loves her, so I told her."

Walter shook his head. "Oh, boy."

"I had to. I don't want Anna to get hurt. She's all I have."

"Where is Anna now?"

"She went home to confront Justin. It's better she know the truth now."

"Of course," Walter said, his arm around her. "You did the right thing."

"What a mess." Marcia wiped her face and looked up at Walter. "I feel like an hour before the wedding he's going to pull out this piece of paper and make Anna sign it. She'll have no choice."

"Anna says that he hasn't approached her about a prenup?"

"That's right. She says he's never even brought it up."

Walter shook his head. "It would be a pretty lowdown thing to do a few days before the wedding."

Marcia leaned her head against Walter's shoulder. "Oh Walter…what am I going to do?"

"All you can do is be there for her."

Marcia looked at him. "I plan on doing that."

"What?"

"Be there, I mean, here, in New Orleans for her."

Walter looked at her in surprise. "Am I hearing you correctly?"

"Yes."

"You're going to move here?"

Marcia nodded. "Yes, for a while. What am I doing in Vermont? All I do is work and come home and work. It's no life at all. I've just been too caught up with my business. Anna is all I have and she's going to need me, whether she goes through with this wedding or not."

"I hope Anna's not the only reason to want to move here."

"No," Marcia said, looking directly at Walter. "I'm in love for the very first time in my life—with you."

Walter pulled her to him. "Oh, Marcia, I was afraid—I was afraid—of losing you. I'm in love with you, too." He lifted her face and when their lips met, it was like magic.

He wiped her face with his fingertips. "Go on in the bathroom and wash your face. You'll feel better."

"All right."

As she walked over to the bathroom, she suddenly saw Walter at the door.

"I hear my phone. I'll be right back."

She washed her face and wiped her eyes with a cold cloth. Her heart felt heavy and she felt queasy in her stomach. She hated it when Anna was upset. She fixed her hair and was just walking out of the bathroom, when Walter ran into the apartment with a cordless phone in his hand.

"It's Richard and has he got some news for us! Here, listen in. Go on, Richard."

Both Marcia and Walter leaned in to hear.

"Well, I took that article, the one that contained the list of slaves and made some calls. I know who your mysterious ghost is."

Marcia was astounded. "You do?"

"Yes," Richard said. "You were both right. Her name was Desiree."

Marcia let out a sigh of relief. At least one part of the mystery was solved. "Go on."

"I found a letter from Mrs. Laura Terhune to her mother, a Mrs. Ida Abernathy. It's dated March 26th 1834. It was kind of hard to read, but the gist of it is that Miss Laura was concerned about the whereabouts of their slave, a woman by the name of Desiree Abernathy."

"Why?"

"It appears that, well, that Desiree was kin to Mrs. Laura Terhune."

"Kin? How do you mean?" Walter asked.

"Mrs. Terhune was born on the plantation, the daughter of a slave owner, but she was an abolitionist at heart. She'd moved up north and married an abolitionist and proceeded to write letters, back and forth to her mother, Ida, requesting freedom for her two sisters. Half sisters."

Marcia understood. "Ah, Aimee and Desiree. They're the daughters of Matthew Abernathy."

"Illegitimate daughters. They were quadroons and Mrs. Terhune wanted them set free so they could attend the quadroon balls and find a man who would take care of them."

"So what happened?"

"It seems Mr. Abernathy refused to set them free, but he also refused to sell them."

"But didn't he buy them back during the slave auction?"

"No, he'd never sold them to Madame LaLaurie. I'm guessing that Desiree, Aimee, and their mother were hired out to work for Madame LaLaurie and the money they made went to him."

"My God. A father treating his own children that way. How could he?" Marcia asked, incredulous.

"There's more," Richard said.

"More? Go on." Walter replied.

"This is exciting. Are you sitting down?"

Both Marcia and Walter moved to the sofa to sit and listen. "We are now," Walter said.

"Mrs. Terhune also received a letter from a Mrs. Hildebrand. She was inquiring about a slave, Tomas, a footman who'd gone missing."

"We know about Tomas. Madame LaLaurie claimed to have sold him because he was too old to work. Maybe he was one of Madame's victims," Walter offered.

Suddenly Marcia thought of the body found in the alley. Could the body in Pirate's Alley have been that of Tomas? Could he have seen something at the mansion and run away to get help?

"She states in her letter to Mrs. Terhune that Madame LaLaurie told her she'd sold Tomas, but refused to say to whom. Mrs. Hildebrand wanted to buy Tomas. But here's the important part…"

"What?" Marcia almost cried out.

"She called Tomas by his nickname—Sam."

Sam!

Marcia let out a sigh of relief. Finally, she had his name. This mysterious Sam was Tomas the footman.

"What the letter states is that Mrs. Hildebrand was going to give him his freedom, but Tomas refused to leave without his love…"

"Desiree!" Marcia and Walter screamed simultaneously.

"Right."

"He wouldn't leave without her, and now she won't leave without him," Marcia said.

"Tomas might have run away to tell someone what he had seen at the LaLaurie Mansion, but I doubt anyone would have believed him. Maybe Madame LaLaurie had him killed," Walter said.

"Could be. But there's more," Richard said in an excited voice.

"Go on."

"The bodies of the slaves that were found during the fire were reburied by the Ursuline nuns at St. Augustine's Catholic Church in 1842."

"So that's where Desiree would be buried?"

"Right."

"But what about Tomas?" Walter asked.

Suddenly Marcia knew where he was—in the garden at LaLaurie Mansion where the ghost had taken her that night! She knew what she had to do to put the slave woman at peace. Find Tomas' bones and have them buried with hers at St. Augustine's Catholic Church.

"Only one place I can think of," Marcia said. "The LaLaurie Mansion."

Walter looked at her in surprise.

"I'll meet you there tomorrow morning," Richard said.

"Thanks for all your help, Richard," Walter said.

They hung up and stared at one another. "Where?" Walter asked her.

"In the garden."

"Are you sure?"

"She showed me."

Walter shook his head and picking up the phone, dialed.

"Who are you calling?"

"The owner. I have to tell him I have to dig up the garden in search of a body. He's not going to be too happy "

"Let's hope we find something, something to let this woman rest in peace."

CHAPTER FOURTEEN

Anna returned to Justin's home and hurried upstairs to his office.

"Justin?" She slowly opened the door and saw that the office was empty. Walking to his desk, she saw a document on the top of his desk. *Please don't let it be what I think.*

Glancing down at the document, she saw that it had PRENUPI-TAL AGREEMENT across the top and a post-it with her name was fastened to the side of the document. *How could he?*

"Looking for me, darling?"

Justin stood at the door, arms crossed, watching her. "Find something interesting there?"

Anna held up the document. "What is this?"

Justin didn't seem at all fazed by her question. "A prenuptial agreement."

"For me to sign?"

"Of course."

"But I thought you loved me."

"I do, but I have to protect my interests."

"I don't want to get married to get divorced, Justin."

Justin walked toward her, but Anna stepped back. "I don't want to divorce you, darling, but sometimes we don't have a choice in the matter."

"Such as if I can't have children?"

Justin hesitated before answering. "Yes. I've been down that road before. I want children and if you can't, well—"

"You'll divorce me."

"Yes."

Anna picked up the document and shook her head, incredulous. Then she removed her engagement ring and walking toward him, threw the ring in his surprised face. "The wedding's off. I'll get my things."

Justin laughed as he picked up the ring from the floor. "What will you do, Anna? You haven't got two pennies to rub together."

"No, I've got something you'll never have."

"Oh? What's that?"

Anna paused in the doorway. "Morals."

The following morning, a team of forensic investigators and the New Orleans Police descended on LaLaurie Mansion. It didn't take long for them to uncover two sets of bones, one female and one male. Marcia thought the female was the young girl who had jumped from the roof in order to escape Madame's wrath. Both were taken to a lab for tests before being taken to St. Augustine's Catholic Church to be buried with Madame LaLaurie's other victims.

Afterwards, Walter and Marcia went upstairs to wait for Anna's call. Marcia was worried because she hadn't heard from Anna the previous night.

"What could have happened? I tried the St. Jean residence, but no one picks up."

"Take it easy, I'm sure she's fine."

But Marcia worried that Justin had somehow wormed his way out of this and was back in Anna's good graces. *Oh please, Let Anna learn the truth about him and see him for what he really is.*

All of a sudden, there were footsteps in the hallway and a knock at the door before Anna walked in. As soon as she saw Marcia, she began to cry.

"I—"

Marcia sat her down on the sofa.

"What happened? Where have you been all night?"

"In a hotel. I couldn't face anyone. I—I've called off the wedding." She pulled a document from her purse. "You were right. There is a prenuptial agreement. Oh, Marcia, I've been so stupid."

Marcia held Anna as she cried. Walter read over the prenup agreement. "Looks like Mr. St. Jean gets a divorce if you can't bear children within the year."

"What?" Marcia asked, incredulous.

"That's what it says."

"Oh, Anna, I'm so sorry, but it's better you found out now."

"I know, but I loved him."

Marcia held Anna as she cried, thankful that Justin. St. Jean was finally out of their lives forever.

After a minute, Anna wiped her eyes. "Justin's right—I'm penniless. What am I going to do? Where am I going to live?"

Marcia looked over at Walter.

"I've been thinking," Walter said as he took Anna's hand. "When I open Flo's Joint, would you mind working for me? You'd have to audition to sing, but I could give you a job waitressing there, as well. It's what I've always wanted to do and it would give you a chance, maybe, of becoming a professional singer."

Anna looked at Walter in surprise. "Really? Are you sure…?"

Walter looked at Marcia. "Yes, I am. I guess I've been afraid of moving on with my life, but life is short."

Marcia turned Anna to face her. "I'm going to move down here and we can live together, like we once did."

Anna hugged her. "Oh, Marcia, thank you. What would I do without you?"

When Anna retreated to the bathroom to wash her face, Walter and Marcia embraced. The future was unknown, but they were together. Being with one another was the most important thing. Marcia shut her eyes, exulting in Walter's embrace. She had finally found the man of her dreams, a wonderful, caring man.

ABOUT THE AUTHOR

Veronica Parker holds an MFA in Creative Writing and graduated cum laude with a degree in English Literature from American University. Her previous novel was *A Heart's Awakening*.

Excerpt from

MISTY BLUE

BY

DYANNE DAVIS

Release Date: May 2006

CHAPTER ONE

Mia's heart stopped. A tiny shiver began at her toes and traveled upward. "Damien," she whispered. She'd reluctantly accompanied Keefe and Ashleigh to the nightclub and had not really been paying attention when the emcee called his name. Nothing could have prepared her for seeing the man she loved living out his dream. And to think she'd almost missed it.

She turned to look at her brother and Ashleigh. "You knew he'd be here, didn't you, Keefe?" For an answer her brother kissed her forehead and held his hand out to Ashleigh, leaving Mia to deal with Damien on her on. He was right to do that. It was about time. A surge of pride filled her as she listened to Damien singing.

"I told you he was good," she murmured as her brother and Ashleigh walked away. Though she spoke to them, her eyes remained fastened on the stage. On Damien.

As the background music played on, Damien began crossing the stage toward her, his eyes never leaving her face. She held her breath. It had been so long, and his face was unreadable. He was giving no indication that he was happy to see her.

Then it happened. On the stage he stopped directly in front of her and smiled, first a tiny little smile that could have been missed. Then the smile took over his entire face until he was grinning broadly. His eyes closed briefly and when they opened, the look he gave her was the same as the one he'd given her the first time she'd seen him and had fallen in love with him—just from the look in his eyes.

As it had been the first time, the look mesmerized her, embraced her, and filled her with things she'd felt for only one man in her entire life-him. Her love was for him. Passion, lust and love tumbled through Mia and again her breath caught in her throat.

Right in front of her, suddenly Damien stopped singing and simply stared at her. Soon the entire audience was looking in her direction, no doubt wondering why the entertainer had stopped singing even though the music continued to play.

"Mia," Damien whispered, for the first time admitting to himself that he'd been afraid she wouldn't come. He'd almost called a dozen times to ask her, but hadn't. He'd been determined not to give in to his feelings for her. Yet he had hoped that she would be there to witness his success. And now she was. And all he wanted in the world was to climb down off that stage, take her in his arms and kiss her, and never let her out of his sight.

As he continued to stare at her, wanting to tell her those things, it finally registered that he wasn't singing. He smiled again at Mia and waited for an answering smile before he resumed singing and turned to walk toward the other end of the stage.

This was it—his moment in the sun. He glanced into the crowd of smiling faces, listened to the women screaming his name. Though it was just as he'd always imagined, the truth of the situation hit him as he sang two more numbers.

None of the attention meant what he'd thought it would. As much as he'd dreamed of a singing career, he wanted something else more. He wanted Mia in his arms. Now, not when the show was over. Now. He smiled at the audience, hoping they would forgive him for what he was about to do. If they didn't…well…so be it.

Damien walked back toward Mia, hardly able to continue singing over the sudden lump constricting his vocal cords.

Mia's attention was riveted on Damien. She didn't want to miss a note. As he sang, her heart soared with love for him. Conflicted, she both wanted the show to go on forever and also to end-so that she could throw herself into his arms, beg him to forgive her, and assure him that she would trust him forever.

When Damien turned and smiled at her again, her heart fluttered erratically and a sudden, intense heat speared her and pooled in her belly. She wanted nothing more than to be in Damien's arms. She needed to warn him not to come any closer but it was too late. He was coming closer and closer, and she was doing everything in her power to remain seated. She didn't want to ruin Damien's opening but God how she wanted to kiss him. He must have had the same thought because a moment before she could whisper, '*No*,' he walked off the stage and stood directly in front of her. In his eyes she saw a question.

"Mia, I love you." Damien said hoarsely. "Can we try again?"

Her eyes shifted automatically to the door her brother had exited through and Damien shifted his body to block her view.

"I don't want Keefe, Mia, I want you."

Her heart soared. She didn't need Keefe's opinion on this one. She'd been given a second chance at loving Damien and she was darn well going to take it.

She flung herself into Damien's arms. "I love you," she murmured into his ear. "Can you ever forgive me?"

He pulled back a little to look at her. "I will if you'll answer my question. You didn't say," he smiled. "Can we start over?" He held her tighter, not wanting to let her go.

"Yes, yes, and yes!" she answered and gave him her entire heart in that moment, without hesitation, without reservation. His lips claimed hers and as the kiss deepened, loud clapping exploded, bringing both of them back to planet Earth. Damien smiled down at her.

"Come on," he urged, taking her hand and pulling her onstage with him. His arm firmly around her, he whispered directions to the band.

He began singing a ballad with music so sweet that each note wrapped around Mia like a warm hug. Then she heard the words, '*Mia, I love you.*' In that instant she realized he'd written the song for her and about her. She was holding back tears as he sang to her as if no one else in the world existed. When he was done, he pulled her to the center of the stage.

"This is Mia," Damien said by way of introduction. "Isn't she beautiful?" Everyone clapped and Damien grinned. "I guess you can all tell that I'm in love with her." Again, the audience went wild.

As much as she wanted to be in Damien's arms, Mia wasn't keen about doing it with an audience. She gave his hand a squeeze and started to walk away, a little afraid that he wouldn't let her off the stage. He followed, kissed her one last time, and released her to return to his singing. She couldn't believe it. She'd almost ruined things, but somehow it had all turned out fine. She smiled as she listened to Damien's deep sultry voice belting out song after song. He'd made it.

"Hi, honey, mind if we join you?"

"Introduce yourself to the girl. She doesn't know us."

Startled, Mia pulled herself together enough to smile at the woman and man who'd just approached her table. She knew instantly who they were. Damien's parents.

"Sure," she answered. She stuck her hand out. "I'm Mia," she said and immediately felt like an idiot. There was not one person in the club that didn't know her name.

"Yes, we know that, Mia," the man answered. "My name's Charles. Charles Terrell. Most everyone calls me Chuck. I'm Damien's old man and this is Kathy, Damien's old lady."

"Damien's mother," Kathy corrected.

"So you're the little piece of…"

"Chuck," Kathy warned.

"That wasn't what I was going to say. So, Mia, you're the little piece of fluff that's been driving Damien crazy all these months? I'd sure like to know what you've got. My son's nose is wide open. And honestly, you don't look at all like what I expected."

Mia felt the smile slipping from her face. Instant compassion for Damien flooded her. For months he'd put up with crap from her brother who until recently had despised him and had done everything in his power to keep her away from him, and at the same time he must have been taking crap at home.

"I beg your pardon," Mia said. "I have no idea what you're talking about."

"Don't listen to Chuck. He's just trying to start trouble. He's only playing with you. Don't take him seriously."

Mia studied them both as she listened to the lilting notes of Damien's song, praying that he would be at her side soon to deal with his parents. She smiled at Kathy but didn't answer.

"Damien told me that you thought you were better than him." Charles continued his attack.

"I never said that, and I never thought it," Mia defended. "There were other things going on in my life that had nothing to do with Damien."

"Yeah, we heard. While you were stringing our son along, you were engaged. We know all of that."

Mia's head snapped toward Charles and she wondered why she was being attacked. This man was almost an exact replica of the man she loved, broad shoulders, beautiful chestnut complexion, a mouth full of white teeth and a killer smile. He didn't, however, have Damien's deep sexy voice, though his own wasn't bad. And he definitely didn't inspire love in her the way his son did. No, on the contrary, what she was feeling for the older man was distaste. There was something slimy about him. While his mouth spoke of her hurting Damien, he'd used his eyes to undress her. She'd felt it as surely as if he'd used his hands and she was disgusted.

"Leave her alone, Chuck."

"I'm just saying I don't see what all the fuss is about. She's just a little slip of a thing. I don't see how she got the boy all twisted up like she did. I want to know her secret. What's the harm in asking her that?"

"It's none of your business."

Mia turned grateful eyes to Kathy before scanning the stage for Damien, praying he would hurry. The show was over but there were still three or four women hanging around him, wanting his autograph, and he was obliging.

"Damien," she whispered, knowing he couldn't possibly hear her. But at that instant he turned and caught her eye and his eyes widened in alarm. She could tell he was rushing through the next autograph.

Then he literally jumped from the stage and came toward her. A sigh of relief escaped Mia. This was one time she was grateful to be rescued. She stood and so did Kathy and Charles.

"Hey, you came. I didn't see you," Damien said to his parents.

"No, I suppose you didn't. Not when you kept looking over this way, at this little girl here."

Again Mia felt dirty. There wasn't anything wrong with the man's words, not even with the way he'd said them. But her skin was crawling all the same.

Damien's arm slid around her and she could almost swear that he was trying to push her behind him.

Damien answered his father's unasked question. "I didn't know Mia was going to be here."

"Then how did she rate a special seat right here in the front while your mother and I were stuck in some funky little corner? And by the way, hot shot, we had to pay to get in."

Charles was poking Damien in the chest with his finger as he punctuated each word. Kathy was biting her lip and Damien looked extremely uncomfortable. Mia was embarrassed for him. She could understand family humiliation. It was her specialty. Her mother had given her a lifetime's worth. Suddenly she noticed something she should have noticed before. Charles was feeling no pain. It was obvious he'd had more than a few drinks.

"How come she rates and we don't? We've been the ones supporting you. She had her ass off somewhere doing God knows what, with whoever. But we know it wasn't you. So why did you reserve a front row seat for her and not us?"

Now it was definitely not her imagination. Damien was positioning his body in front of hers. He was trying to protect her. Instead of feeling the intense annoyance and aversion for his father she had felt a moment before, Mia felt a surge of love for Damien.

"I'll pay for your admission and your drinks. Just tell me what you spent."

The emotion in Damien's voice was pure exasperation. Mia was extremely familiar with that tone.

"Fifty dollars, admission and drinks." Kathy looked at her son and smiled weakly.

Mia watched as Damien's hand went to his pocket.

"How the hell would you know? Did you pay for anything?" Charles interrupted. "It was a hundred."

Observing this family situation from behind Damien, Mia saw Damien tighten his jaw. She also saw as he counted out the money and handed it to his father that he didn't have anything left in his wallet.

"Now that you have your money, can I please give the two of you a proper introduction? Mia, my parents, my mother, Kathy Morrison, and my father, Charles Terrell." He continued before anyone else got the chance to speak, "No, they're not divorced. They were never married. Sorry, Pop, I just thought I'd beat you to it."

He kissed his mother's cheek and Mia watched the woman's eyes as they became veiled. Damien had never spoken a lot about his parents, just that he'd moved back home with his mother. His father, he hadn't mentioned.

"I told her to call me Chuck."

"You hate it when anyone calls you Chuck." For a moment Damien stared at his father in disbelief, then recovered. "Come on, everyone, let's sit down," Damien said.

"I still want to know how she rates a front row table," Charles said as he crumpled Damien's money and put it in his pocket.

"Ashleigh asked me to reserve a table. I did."

"You're banging them both?"

Damien leaned over and whispered to his father and when he pulled away, the man looked Mia over, a slight sneer on his face.

"I'm sorry, Mia. It seems my son thinks I've offended you. Perhaps I was wrong in my assessment of you. Maybe you didn't think you were too good for Damien."

He turned from Mia to glare at his son. "Maybe it's my son who's gotten weak since he moved back home with his mama." A huge scowl replaced the sneer. "Man, this woman's got you whipped. I warned you about that." He then turned his glare on Kathy. "So you finally got your way. You managed to turn my son into a freaking mama's boy. Well, if I have any say about it and you know I always have," he laughed crudely, "I'm going to see to it that he changes back."

Charles laughed at Mia. "Enjoy this while you can because I'm going to go find my son's balls. And when I do, I'm going to give them back to him and he's going to start acting like a man again, no more pulling some woman on the stage and singing to her, telling the whole damn audience that he's in love with her." He glared at Damien. "Do you think I ever did that with your mother? Hell, no!"

Mia watched as Kathy winced noticeably, as though she'd been hit. "I don't—

"I agree with Mia," Damien said, interrupting her, turning to look at her, pleading with his eyes. "I don't think now's the time for this."

"Makes me no never mind," Charles retorted. "I'm outta here."

"Chuck," Kathy stood. "How am I supposed to get home?"

The look he gave her turned what before had been only dislike into something worse for Mia.

"Don't worry, Kathy, I'll take you home," Mia volunteered, ignoring the fact that her brother Keefe had brought her and she was herself without a ride home. Still, Damien's father needed someone to wipe that look off his face and Damien's mother needed an ally.

"Don't worry, Mom, I'll take you home." Damien kissed his mother's cheek and pulled Mia into his arms. "I'm so sorry. My pops had a few drinks. Will you please wait for me? I have another show."

"I'll wait." Mia smiled at his look of doubt. "I don't have a ride home either." She watched as he grinned, then retook the stage.

She sat down, barely glancing at Kathy. "Would you like something to…to…eat," she asked, changing her mind about asking the woman if she could buy her a drink. She didn't think she wanted to talk to anyone else tonight who'd been drinking.

"Thanks, Mia, but I'm fine."

Mia looked up and found Kathy studying her, a strange look on her face. "Is something wrong?" she asked, praying she was not opening herself up to attack by another of Damien's parents.

"I love my son," Kathy began, "but I'm wondering why you're with him. I can understand why you broke it off but to do it again…" She tsked. "He's going to hurt you, Mia. He can't help it. He's just like his father."

Like father like son. Like mother like daughter. Mia had more in common with Damien than she'd ever realized. It was in that moment that her heart broke for him and it was also in that moment that she determined that she would mend both their hearts, attend their hurts. Damien was nothing like his father and she was nothing like her mother.

"Kathy, don't worry. Damien is not Charles. He loves me."

"He's my son, but he's a dog just like his father. He couldn't be true to you if you paid him."

"But he has been."

"That's because he didn't have you. You confused him. He didn't know how to react."

"Why are you saying this?" Mia asked, puzzled.

"Because I don't want you to get hurt." Kathy's eyes wandered toward the door. "I'm not doing this to be mean."

"You don't believe Damien loves me?"

"He does for now, until he gets what he wants, then…" She shrugged her shoulders. "I think his love will fade and you'll be all alone and heartsick. With luck maybe you'll have one thing to remember him by. A baby, a blessing and a curse."

Mia took Kathy's hand. "It's not going to happen, not to us. Damien loves me and I love him. You have no idea of the obstacles we've overcome to get here."

"I know."

Mia watched as Kathy laughed softly. She was getting a sick feeling in the pit of her stomach and wished that the woman would just stop talking. But by the intense look on her face, Mia knew that wasn't likely to happen.

"I know him a hell of a lot better than you and I've known him for a whole lot longer. I birthed him. When he gets what he wants, I promise you he will throw you to the side. The two of them are just

alike. They're two peas in a pod. That might be a cliché, but it's true
" She nodded again toward the door. "That's Damien in twenty more
years. Look at me and you'll see yourself in twenty years if you stay
with him."

Mia stared at Kathy, then shook her head and looked toward the
stage. Kathy was wrong. *Ignore her*, she ordered her mind. Her future
with Damien would be whatever they made it.

A LOVER'S LEGACY

2006 Publication Schedule

January

A Lover's Legacy	Love Lasts Forever	Under the Cherry
Veronica Parker	Dominiqua Douglas	Moon
1-58571-167-5	1-58571-187-X	Christal Jordan-Mims
$9.95	$9.95	1-58571-169-1
		$12.95

February

Second Chances at Love	Enchanted Desire	Caught Up
Cheris Hodges	Wanda Thomas	Deatri King Bey
1-58571-188-8	1-58571-176-4	1-58571-178-0
$9.95	$9.95	$12.95

March

I'm Gonna Make You	Through The Fire	Notes When Summer
Love Me	Seressia Glass	Ends
Gwyneth Bolton	1-58571-173-X	Beverly Lauderdale
1-58571-181-0	$9.95	1-58571-180-2
$9.95		$12.95

April

Sin and Surrender	Unearthing Passions	Between Tears
J.M. Jeffries	Elaine Sims	Pamela Ridley
1-58571-189-6	1-58571-184-5	1-58571-179-0
$9.95	$9.95	$12.95

May

Misty Blue	Ironic	Cricket's Serenade
Dyanne Davis	Pamela Leigh Starr	Carolita Blythe
1-58571-186-1	1-58571-168-3	1-58571-183-7
$9.95	$9.95	$12.95

June

Cupid	Havana Sunrise	Bound For Mt. Zion
Barbara Keaton	Kymberly Hunt	Chris Parker
1-58571-174-8	1-58571-182-9	1-58571-191-8
$9.95	$9.95	$12.95

2006 Publication Schedule (continued)

July

Love Me Carefully	No Ordinary Love	Rehoboth Road
A.C. Arthur	Angela Weaver	Anita Ballard-Jones
1-58571-177-2	1-58571-198-5	1-58571-196-9
$9.95	$9.95	$12.95

August

Scent of Rain	Love in High Gear	Rise of the Phoenix
Annetta P. Lee	Charlotte Roy	Kenneth Whetstone
158571-199-3	158571-185-3	1-58571-197-7
$9.95	$9.95	$12.95

September

The Business of Love	Rock Star	A Dead Man Speaks
Cheris Hodges	Rosyln Hardy Holcomb	Lisa Jones Johnson
1-58571-193-4	1-58571-200-0	1-58571-203-5
$9.95	$9.95	$12.95

October

Who's That Lady	A Dangerous Woman	Sinful Intentions
Andrea Jackson	J.M. Jeffries	Crystal Rhodes
1-58571-190-X	1-58571-195-0	1-58571-201-9
$9.95	$9.95	$12.95

November

Only You	Ebony Eyes	By and By
Crystal Hubbard	Kei Swanson	Collette Haywood
1-58571-208-6	1-58571-194-2	1-58571-209-4
$9.95	$9.95	$12.95

December

Let's Get It On	Nights Over Egypt	A Pefect Place to Pray
Dyanne Davis	Barbara Keaton	Ikesha Goodwin
1-58571-210-8	1-58571-192-6	1-58571-202-7
$9.95	$9.95	$12.95

Other Genesis Press, Inc. Titles

A Dangerous Deception	J.M. Jeffries	$8.95
A Dangerous Love	J.M. Jeffries	$8.95
A Dangerous Obsession	J.M. Jeffries	$8.95
A Drummer's Beat to Mend	Kei Swanson	$9.95
A Happy Life	Charlotte Harris	$9.95
A Heart's Awakening	Veronica Parker	$9.95
A Lark on the Wing	Phyliss Hamilton	$9.95
A Love of Her Own	Cheris F. Hodges	$9.95
A Love to Cherish	Beverly Clark	$8.95
A Risk of Rain	Dar Tomlinson	$8.95
A Twist of Fate	Beverly Clark	$8.95
A Will to Love	Angie Daniels	$9.95
Acquisitions	Kimberley White	$8.95
Across	Carol Payne	$12.95
After the Vows	Leslie Esdaile	$10.95
(Summer Anthology)	T.T. Henderson	
	Jacqueline Thomas	
Again My Love	Kayla Perrin	$10.95
Against the Wind	Gwynne Forster	$8.95
All I Ask	Barbara Keaton	$8.95
Ambrosia	T.T. Henderson	$8.95
An Unfinished Love Affair	Barbara Keaton	$8.95
And Then Came You	Dorothy Elizabeth Love	$8.95
Angel's Paradise	Janice Angelique	$9.95
At Last	Lisa G. Riley	$8.95
Best of Friends	Natalie Dunbar	$8.95
Beyond the Rapture	Beverly Clark	$9.95
Blaze	Barbara Keaton	$9.95
Blood Lust	J. M. Jeffries	$9.95
Bodyguard	Andrea Jackson	$9.95
Boss of Me	Diana Nyad	$8.95
Bound by Love	Beverly Clark	$8.95
Breeze	Robin Hampton Allen	$10.95

Other Genesis Press, Inc. Titles (continued)

Broken	Dar Tomlinson	$24.95
By Design	Barbara Keaton	$8.95
Cajun Heat	Charlene Berry	$8.95
Careless Whispers	Rochelle Alers	$8.95
Cats & Other Tales	Marilyn Wagner	$8.95
Caught in a Trap	Andre Michelle	$8.95
Caught Up In the Rapture	Lisa G. Riley	$9.95
Cautious Heart	Cheris F Hodges	$8.95
Chances	Pamela Leigh Starr	$8.95
Cherish the Flame	Beverly Clark	$8.95
Class Reunion	Irma Jenkins/John Brown	$12.95
Code Name: Diva	J.M. Jeffries	$9.95
Conquering Dr. Wexler's Heart	Kimberley White	$9.95
Crossing Paths, Tempting Memories	Dorothy Elizabeth Love	$9.95
Cypress Whisperings	Phyllis Hamilton	$8.95
Dark Embrace	Crystal Wilson Harris	$8.95
Dark Storm Rising	Chinelu Moore	$10.95
Daughter of the Wind	Joan Xian	$8.95
Deadly Sacrifice	Jack Kean	$22.95
Designer Passion	Dar Tomlinson	$8.95
Dreamtective	Liz Swados	$5.95
Ebony Butterfly II	Delilah Dawson	$14.95
Echoes of Yesterday	Beverly Clark	$9.95
Eden's Garden	Elizabeth Rose	$8.95
Everlastin' Love	Gay G. Gunn	$8.95
Everlasting Moments	Dorothy Elizabeth Love	$8.95
Everything and More	Sinclair Lebeau	$8.95
Everything but Love	Natalie Dunbar	$8.95
Eve's Prescription	Edwina Martin Arnold	$8.95
Falling	Natalie Dunbar	$9.95
Fate	Pamela Leigh Starr	$8.95
Finding Isabella	A.J. Garrotto	$8.95

A LOVER'S LEGACY

Other Genesis Press, Inc. Titles (continued)

Forbidden Quest	Dar Tomlinson	$10.95
Forever Love	Wanda Thomas	$8.95
From the Ashes	Kathleen Suzanne	$8.95
	Jeanne Sumerix	
Gentle Yearning	Rochelle Alers	$10.95
Glory of Love	Sinclair LeBeau	$10.95
Go Gentle into that Good Night	Malcom Boyd	$12.95
Goldengroove	Mary Beth Craft	$16.95
Groove, Bang, and Jive	Steve Cannon	$8.99
Hand in Glove	Andrea Jackson	$9.95
Hard to Love	Kimberley White	$9.95
Hart & Soul	Angie Daniels	$8.95
Heartbeat	Stephanie Bedwell-Grime	$8.95
Hearts Remember	M. Loui Quezada	$8.95
Hidden Memories	Robin Allen	$10.95
Higher Ground	Leah Latimer	$19.95
Hitler, the War, and the Pope	Ronald Rychiak	$26.95
How to Write a Romance	Kathryn Falk	$18.95
I Married a Reclining Chair	Lisa M. Fuhs	$8.95
Indigo After Dark Vol. I	Nia Dixon/Angelique	$10.95
Indigo After Dark Vol. II	Dolores Bundy/Cole Riley	$10.95
Indigo After Dark Vol. III	Montana Blue/Coco Morena	$10.95
Indigo After Dark Vol. IV	Cassandra Colt/	$14.95
	Diana Richeaux	
Indigo After Dark Vol. V	Delilah Dawson	$14.95
Icie	Pamela Leigh Starr	$8.95
I'll Be Your Shelter	Giselle Carmichael	$8.95
I'll Paint a Sun	A.J. Garrotto	$9.95
Illusions	Pamela Leigh Starr	$8.95
Indiscretions	Donna Hill	$8.95
Intentional Mistakes	Michele Sudler	$9.95
Interlude	Donna Hill	$8.95
Intimate Intentions	Angie Daniels	$8.95

Other Genesis Press, Inc. Titles (continued)

Jolie's Surrender	Edwina Martin-Arnold	$8.95
Kiss or Keep	Debra Phillips	$8.95
Lace	Giselle Carmichael	$9.95
Last Train to Memphis	Elsa Cook	$12.95
Lasting Valor	Ken Olsen	$24.95
Let Us Prey	Hunter Lundy	$25.95
Life Is Never As It Seems	J.J. Michael	$12.95
Lighter Shade of Brown	Vicki Andrews	$8.95
Love Always	Mildred E. Riley	$10.95
Love Doesn't Come Easy	Charlyne Dickerson	$8.95
Love Unveiled	Gloria Greene	$10.95
Love's Deception	Charlene Berry	$10.95
Love's Destiny	M. Loui Quezada	$8.95
Mae's Promise	Melody Walcott	$8.95
Magnolia Sunset	Giselle Carmichael	$8.95
Matters of Life and Death	Lesego Malepe, Ph.D.	$15.95
Meant to Be	Jeanne Sumerix	$8.95
Midnight Clear	Leslie Esdaile	$10.95
(Anthology)	Gwynne Forster	
	Carmen Green	
	Monica Jackson	
Midnight Magic	Gwynne Forster	$8.95
Midnight Peril	Vicki Andrews	$10.95
Misconceptions	Pamela Leigh Starr	$9.95
Montgomery's Children	Richard Perry	$14.95
My Buffalo Soldier	Barbara B. K. Reeves	$8.95
Naked Soul	Gwynne Forster	$8.95
Next to Last Chance	Louisa Dixon	$24.95
No Apologies	Seressia Glass	$8.95
No Commitment Required	Seressia Glass	$8.95
No Regrets	Mildred E. Riley	$8.95
Nowhere to Run	Gay G. Gunn	$10.95
O Bed! O Breakfast!	Rob Kuehnle	$14.95

Other Genesis Press, Inc. Titles (continued)

Object of His Desire	A. C. Arthur	$8.95
Office Policy	A. C. Arthur	$9.95
Once in a Blue Moon	Dorianne Cole	$9.95
One Day at a Time	Bella McFarland	$8.95
Outside Chance	Louisa Dixon	$24.95
Passion	T.T. Henderson	$10.95
Passion's Blood	Cherif Fortin	$22.95
Passion's Journey	Wanda Thomas	$8.95
Past Promises	Jahmel West	$8.95
Path of Fire	T.T. Henderson	$8.95
Path of Thorns	Annetta P. Lee	$9.95
Peace Be Still	Colette Haywood	$12.95
Picture Perfect	Reon Carter	$8.95
Playing for Keeps	Stephanie Salinas	$8.95
Pride & Joi	Gay G. Gunn	$15.95
Pride & Joi	Gay G. Gunn	$8.95
Promises to Keep	Alicia Wiggins	$8.95
Quiet Storm	Donna Hill	$10.95
Reckless Surrender	Rochelle Alers	$6.95
Red Polka Dot in a World of Plaid	Varian Johnson	$12.95
Reluctant Captive	Joyce Jackson	$8.95
Rendezvous with Fate	Jeanne Sumerix	$8.95
Revelations	Cheris F. Hodges	$8.95
Rivers of the Soul	Leslie Esdaile	$8.95
Rocky Mountain Romance	Kathleen Suzanne	$8.95
Rooms of the Heart	Donna Hill	$8.95
Rough on Rats and Tough on Cats	Chris Parker	$12.95
Secret Library Vol. 1	Nina Sheridan	$18.95
Secret Library Vol. 2	Cassandra Colt	$8.95
Shades of Brown	Denise Becker	$8.95
Shades of Desire	Monica White	$8.95

Other Genesis Press, Inc. Titles (continued)

Shadows in the Moonlight	Jeanne Sumerix	$8.95
Sin	Crystal Rhodes	$8.95
So Amazing	Sinclair LeBeau	$8.95
Somebody's Someone	Sinclair LeBeau	$8.95
Someone to Love	Alicia Wiggins	$8.95
Song in the Park	Martin Brant	$15.95
Soul Eyes	Wayne L. Wilson	$12.95
Soul to Soul	Donna Hill	$8.95
Southern Comfort	J.M. Jeffries	$8.95
Still the Storm	Sharon Robinson	$8.95
Still Waters Run Deep	Leslie Esdaile	$8.95
Stories to Excite You	Anna Forrest/Divine	$14.95
Subtle Secrets	Wanda Y. Thomas	$8.95
Suddenly You	Crystal Hubbard	$9.95
Sweet Repercussions	Kimberley White	$9.95
Sweet Tomorrows	Kimberly White	$8.95
Taken by You	Dorothy Elizabeth Love	$9.95
Tattooed Tears	T. T. Henderson	$8.95
The Color Line	Lizzette Grayson Carter	$9.95
The Color of Trouble	Dyanne Davis	$8.95
The Disappearance of Allison Jones	Kayla Perrin	$5.95
The Honey Dipper's Legacy	Pannell-Allen	$14.95
The Joker's Love Tune	Sidney Rickman	$15.95
The Little Pretender	Barbara Cartland	$10.95
The Love We Had	Natalie Dunbar	$8.95
The Man Who Could Fly	Bob & Milana Beamon	$18.95
The Missing Link	Charlyne Dickerson	$8.95
The Price of Love	Sinclair LeBeau	$8.95
The Smoking Life	Ilene Barth	$29.95
The Words of the Pitcher	Kei Swanson	$8.95
Three Wishes	Seressia Glass	$8.95
Ties That Bind	Kathleen Suzanne	$8.95
Tiger Woods	Libby Hughes	$5.95

Other Genesis Press, Inc. Titles (continued)

Time is of the Essence	Angie Daniels	$9.95
Timeless Devotion	Bella McFarland	$9.95
Tomorrow's Promise	Leslie Esdaile	$8.95
Truly Inseparable	Wanda Y. Thomas	$8.95
Unbreak My Heart	Dar Tomlinson	$8.95
Uncommon Prayer	Kenneth Swanson	$9.95
Unconditional	A.C. Arthur	$9.95
Unconditional Love	Alicia Wiggins	$8.95
Until Death Do Us Part	Susan Paul	$8.95
Vows of Passion	Bella McFarland	$9.95
Wedding Gown	Dyanne Davis	$8.95
What's Under Benjamin's Bed	Sandra Schaffer	$8.95
When Dreams Float	Dorothy Elizabeth Love	$8.95
Whispers in the Night	Dorothy Elizabeth Love	$8.95
Whispers in the Sand	LaFlorya Gauthier	$10.95
Wild Ravens	Altonya Washington	$9.95
Yesterday Is Gone	Beverly Clark	$10.95
Yesterday's Dreams, Tomorrow's Promises	Reon Laudat	$8.95
Your Precious Love	Sinclair LeBeau	$8.95

Order Form

Mail to: Genesis Press, Inc.
P.O. Box 101
Columbus, MS 39703

Name _____

Address _____

City/State _____ Zip _____

Telephone _____

Ship to (if different from above)

Name _____

Address _____

City/State _____ Zip _____

Telephone _____

Credit Card Information

Credit Card # _____ ☐ Visa ☐ Mastercard

Expiration Date (mm/yy) _____ ☐ AmEx ☐ Discover

Qty.	Author	Title	Price	Total

Use this order form, or call **1-888-INDIGO-1**	**Total for books** _____ **Shipping and handling:** $5 first two books, $1 each additional book _____ **Total S & H** _____ **Total amount enclosed** _____ *Mississippi residents add 7% sales tax*

Visit www.genesis-press.com for latest releases and excerpts.